CU00842415

A Man, a Machine, and the Thing in the Dark

A Man, a Machine, and the Thing in the Dark

Evan Aster Reed

Evan Aster Reed

ISBN-13: 978-1-7364373-1-5

Cover design by: Maxim Mitenkov

For those who have seen the depths, and for those who have, unknowingly, reached in to pull them out.

WARNING

This book contains themes that may be sensitive to some readers. Discretion is advised

CONTENTS

CONTENTS

1

Don't Turn Around

Don't turn around. Just don't do it. Camden felt a breath on his neck and knew it would take him if he looked back. Nails grazed up his bicep, demanding a reaction, but he stayed still. He knew what it wanted, and it would not get him. The darkness called out to him, as it always did, but it had never been so close, so demanding with its presence. Camden's heartbeat was audible to both himself and the creature behind him. "Just a brief look. Just a single glance, dear Cam," it whispered in his ear with the seductive voice of the devil. A shiver ran up his spine as a clench in his gut turned him inside out. It could not make him; that was his only solace. Camden had to turn around, of his own free will, and he would not. "Come with me ..." The voice echoed in the abyss as a wave.

"No," Camden replied, "I don't need you."

A chuckle made his vision blur and his stomach clench. "Is that so?" it said as a clawed hand wrapped around his neck. Fingers reached up his cheek to scrape delicately against the skin. Everything was spinning as he teetered on his feet, unsure of his own footing. If he passed out, did that count as giving in? Camden couldn't faint. He would not. The claws pried his mouth open and dug into his throat. He had visions of spiders crawling inside, but he could not react. If he responded, it would know. "Come with me." It leaned its head, or wherever the sound was coming from, next to Camden's. Camden squeezed his eyes closed. The claws raked against the back of his throat, and he retched. At the reaction, it withdrew, leaving nails trailing along his teeth. Then it pressed a claw against his tongue, drawing from the back toward the tip, drawing blood. The claws ran along his teeth, clacking softly along the indents between them. The hand pulled to run along his lips, painting them with blood. The fingers traced along the contours of his face, memorizing every feature, every crevice.

"No," Camden said. "Go away. Go away. *Go away!*"

His voice should've echoed out in the blackness from which they stood. The endless surroundings should have answered back, but it ate his cries. The shadows watched silently, giving him the sense of being locked in a box to suffocate. That's what this place always held: a thickness of air and a promise of endlessness.

One spindly hand pressed against his forehead and yanked his head back. His neck, now splayed before the creature to explore, felt strained against the hold. Had it always been able to manipulate him so? Was it getting more powerful? It leaned over to press its face into his stretched neck. A tongue squished against the skin over his artery as if it could taste his pulse. A shudder rippled through every nerve in Camden's body. His vision cleared and then blurred again with an intense ache building in his gut. He gasped as it whispered into his neck, "I can show you everything. You can have everything. Just come with me."

"No," he said. Was he losing the will to fight? No, he couldn't afford to lose will. The second hand grabbed Camden's wrist to twist behind his back. There was no way it had this much control. With him incapacitated, it moved its face into his shoulder and inhaled. A sharper sensation pierced his abdomen as its tongue pressed into skin to sample him. It growled as it raked sharp teeth along his neck, not breaking skin. The creature hissed. As it tightened its grip on his wrist, it yanked up. Camden cried out. His shoulder screamed. "No." It came out a whimper, almost a plea.

The other hand drew across his cheek, "Oh my, where did all that fight go? I won't hurt you if you come with me."

"No," Camden begged.

Fingers traced his neck, halting at the trapezius. They dug like a drill into the soft tissue above the collarbone. Camden screamed and stomped his legs, but the other hand held him in place. As they dug more extensively through the muscle, dodging the bones, Camden spasmed.

"Please!" Camden cried. "No."

"Shh, shh," It hushed in his ear as it grabbed hold of something attached to bone. It rubbed its cheek against his. Camden's breath came out choppy as the pain caused his lungs to seize. All the fight left Camden's body. He went limp, gasping. "It can all stop if you just come with me."

Camden whimpered through choked cries, "Why? Why are you doing this to me?"

The hand withdrew from his chest cavity and laid wet claws on his face, holding his head against the side of its own. "Because I want you, Cam. I want everything you are." Camden's legs wobbled as he tried to regain his footing. "Why do you torture me this way? Stop keeping me at arm's length. It's so terribly rude."

Camden breathed for several moments as the bloody hand held him stable. It could hurt him. It wanted to hurt him, and he didn't stand a chance. The absolution and confident movements of the creature crumbled his own indecision. Would it be better to give in? "I—" Gasp. "I don't want—"

A lump bounced in his stomach, as if someone were walloping him. Everything spun while the hands held him firm. His body collapsed into the arms of the creature as he spewed semisolid matter in front of them. It flicked its sharp tongue to graze his ear, sharp teeth pressed against the lobe. Needles prodded the skin as the creature wavered. Camden could feel it debating whether to tear it from his head. It let go and said, "I can help you. I can free you."

"Nnngghh." The grip on his arm loosened, and Camden dipped forward, only for the second hand to grab his other wrist. He slid to his knees. A foot pressed to his back. "No ... please. No more."

"Come with me." It was the last offer.

He knelt at the complete mercy of the impatient creature, arms held behind him. With the last of his determination, he shook his head. Crack. Crack. Camden cried. The pain was insurmountable. Every part of his torso screamed as his arms ripped from their sockets. Ears ringing, he collapsed into the pile of vomit; eyes unfocused, they stared off to the side. If he had a chance to run away at any point, it was too late.

The creature leaned over him to whisper in his ear. The breath gave him goosebumps. It was right out of sight. "You think I can't have you, but you have too much faith in what you believe."

It placed its talons on his torn shoulders and flipped him upward. Camden wept from the jarring forcefulness of the movement, yet still kept his head facing away. The fingers twisted through his hair, traced his jaw's features, and pressed against his neck. Still he would not look. He hissed as it pressed the pads of its fingers against the open wound on his shoulder. It leaned in, pressing its lips against the wound, digging its tongue into it. Camden flinched. As it drew back with an exasperated sigh, it groaned, smacking its lips. Leaning closer, it shook with anticipation.

"Cam," it whispered, "come with me."

And it took hold of his head, forcing him to see it. Camden's heart wrenched as he looked upon the demon that had tortured and terrified him. It was his mirror image. "No," he managed. The creature's face, *his* face, opened up to reveal rows of dangerous teeth. A spiked tongue flicked out to catch stray drool. The pit of teeth and salivating vibrated with excitement. Inches from taking his head, it backed and closed its mouth, shaking still.

"Oh?" His face smiled back at him as the creature spoke with Camden's own mouth, "Still got some of that annoying fight left?"

Camden blinked tired eyes up at it. Arms dangled beside him. Still, if these were his last moments, he wanted to have one final say. "You can't have me." He tried to smile, but he wasn't sure if it was possible.

His own face stared with the contortion of chagrin. It broke out into tremors as it gripped him hard with its sharp claws. Camden gave a squeak as his shoulders explained the pain to his torso. Sharp teeth ground against each other, eyebrows creased, and in an instant of passion, it snapped off his head. After chewing, it let out a sadistic growl and said, "Says who?"

2

Fear the Abyss

The creature let out a cry that faded into nothing. Thick blood coasted along the fluid ground, and its body twitched involuntarily. It grabbed its head, shaking as it backed away. *It didn't just do that.* Deeper into the darkness of the abyss, it walked until no headless body lay mocking, a hollowness carried it onward. It dragged its fingered feet along the lightless ground. Beneath its feet, the ground rippled as if made of water. The reflection in the abyss came from nowhere and everywhere at once. Objects within seemed to be lit in daylight, while the absence of such was darker than a moonless night. It was home. A place where it could go when emptiness took hold.

The creature found him here, though not always. The boy, the man, walked about aimlessly, searching for anything and seeing things in this absence. Unlike him, the creature found what it looked for, and it reached for him. With blood on the black claws, the creature clenched its grip.

There was another. The gaze of something else fell upon it from somewhere within the abyss. In the pure darkness, its eyes fell upon her facing away. They looked just like him, but a female of his kind. She faced away, and the creature wondered if it could play with this one too. It reached out a dripping hand to grab her shoulder. Inches away. She spun and grabbed its wrist in a vise. Her eyes, missing color, pierced through its very being. It shrank back, tugging its arm against the hold. Her eyes narrowed as she spoke. "You still wear his face."

It froze at the mention of him. *Did she know him?* It wanted to see her expression, but nothing inside let itself gaze upon her eyes. It hissed at her as it tried to pry free its wrist, but she was immovable in every sense.

"Look at me," she said, and it complied. The skin beside her eyes crinkled as she grimaced. She grabbed the hair on its head tightly. "I see you." The words echoed around it—strength zapping from its insides. The darkness melted away, revealing the creature it truly was. The illusion of the human face dissolved, revealing what she saw. Her eyes looked with judgment. "How dare you take something of mine."

The creature whimpered as it folded in on itself. She knelt down to it and slackened her grip. With her other hand, she stroked its true face. Her eyes softened, and it found it could look at her—now.

"Now—" she said with nary an echo. The surrounding space closed in and held the sound close. "Why don't you just return what you stole?" It did not understand her. What was she referring to? What did it have that she wanted? What had it taken? Upon seeing the confusion, she pressed a finger to its temple, bringing flashes of Camden's face to the surface of its mind. It shook its head. Her eyes darkened, causing the creature to squirm. It nodded. She smiled at the change in decision. "Good," she said.

She grabbed its jaws and pried them open, splitting the creature's face to show its layers of razor-sharp teeth. Without hesitation, she dug her arm deep into it to rummage for something. It felt her hand tug and pull at the strange places within its gut. Then she withdrew her hand, holding a sludge of black, inky substance. It dripped down her arm like black honey. She flicked at it with her fingers, and the liquid substance fragmented off and fell away like dust. She eyed the object she held, and the creature closed its mouth, thankful for the lack of attention. The object in her hand reflected light at different angles. It looked like a shard of a thick mirror. Every side reflected a light nonexistent within the darkness of the abyss. Pressing it to her lips, she kissed and then let it go. The pure white shard flickered out of the abyss as if it hadn't existed, taking the refracting light with it.

Those sharp eyes cast one last dark glance at the creature balled beneath her. She said, "Touch anything of mine again, and I will remove you."

As she walked into the darkness, the abyss bent around her. The creature pressed its face into the inky blackness of the ground below and whimpered. This place was not home. This was hers, and it had just assumed it belonged here. She wasn't just the darkness; she was the abyss itself.

Somewhere else, Camden sat upright, gripping his head over and over to make sure it wasn't missing, baffled that he was alive. He had sweated through his bedsheets, and his heart pounded in his ears as he made sense of his surrounding reality.

3

Therapy

"I had a dream the other night," Camden said after the room had been quiet for a few moments. "I died, but I still remember the fear."

"Dreams aren't real, Camden," his psychiatrist said in dismissal. Some topics Dr. Morgan avoided because he feared particular unknowns. Camden didn't look at him, but he knew the psychiatrist's vocal tells. They had known each other for years since Camden's friend died in some freak accident that both emotionally scarred him and dragged him into a dark depression. At first, Dr. Morgan seemed kind, caring, and a good listener, but after a few months, the truth of him turned out to be abrasive, arrogant, and apathetic. As months turned into years, Camden had learned everything about the man sitting across from him. He knew that Morgan spoke abruptly when avoidant, his foot bounced if uninterested, he took his whiskey neat, and that above anything else, he adored patronizing Camden.

When Morgan initially poked at his fleshy bits, he hadn't been aware, but after a few insurgent fits of rage, he noticed that glint in the doctor's eyes. Of course, Camden would be unlucky enough to get paired with a sadistic psychiatrist. Then again, weren't all psychiatrists a little sadistic? He wasn't sure. He only knew Dr. Morgan. The doctor watched him, but Camden's eyes flicked everywhere else around the spacious minimalist retreat of a room. Meticulous about only certain things being visible to his patients, he created an empty vibe that included spotless wood floors, two magnetic chairs, his desk in the corner with little on it, a bookshelf on the far wall that held a particular array of psych books, and an entire wall of glass windows that peered down into the daunting city. From where they sat, only the taller buildings could be seen. The street couldn't be seen from the thirty-second floor. A cloudy day with the gray clouds brought in the same dull colors. Mechatronic birds zipped by, doing surveillance of which windows needed cleaning or if any need replacing. Artificial intelligence running on its own allowed for better management of everything. Anything scanned, they processed; if tax funding did not match up, they changed it accordingly.

Morgan spun his pen to get Camden's attention. Eyes twitched at that annoying habit. Dark-gray eyes stared unblinking at him, and Camden stared back. Morgan didn't look as horrendous as his personality, with features almost gentle. Downturned eyes, a round nose, and well-kept dark hair gelled back completed his look. Despite his demeanor, the doctor had a primal instinct that always pushed Camden up and over the edge. The doctor's patience must have run out, because he said, "This dream must have bothered you."

Camden smirked internally. As much as Camden distrusted his doctor, he enjoyed annoying Morgan. Despite Morgan's disgust with dream interpretation and claims it wasn't science, Camden wanted to hear him struggle to make sense of the horrors he faced last night. Now was Morgan's turn to wiggle under the microscope.

Dr. Morgan sat relaxed in his modern chair, his left leg over his right, revealing perfect leather shoes that hadn't touched dirt in their entire lifetime. His suit pants shifted upon his leg, showing tightly pulled socks. A matching dark vest eased over his wrinkle-free button-down shirt. A yellow notebook sat open in his lap, and he tapped it with his matte-black laser pen. He had stopped using a holo-tablet at some point and seemed to go through those journals regularly. Each journal, color coded by year, spanned through a rainbow on the bookshelf, and Camden's session novels completed the entire array. Morgan preferred to keep a clean-shaven face, while Camden opted to grow a beard. Or at least try. It always turned out splotchy and irregular, so he kept it short. Still, Camden waited for his doctor to break down his dream, but Morgan seemed torn. He twisted his lips to chew his cheek, but Camden doubted he did so. He spun his pen again, and Camden couldn't help an involuntary squirm. The glint in the doctor's eye was palpable. This controlling factor allowed Morgan to untense and give in to Camden's wishes. "Well, some believe dreams are our mind's way of releasing pent-up energy. In this dream, how did you die?"

"A creature attacked and ate me. It had my face," Camden said, regarding the psychiatrist's twitching eye. He tried to repress a dumb smile that would give away the game. They were always fighting each other over the conversations. Every step of the way, Morgan pushed him, and every step of the way, Camden would fight him. Whoever had control of topics had the advantage. It was a tireless war, but Camden preferred it to the questions Morgan brought up. They always had some hidden agenda that resulted in a mental breakdown on Camden's part. He tried not to let Morgan take control of the session for that exact reason.

He spun the pen, eliciting another annoyed shudder from Camden, uncrossed his legs to lean forward, taking the general position when he lectured, "Freud said that dreams represent wishes that you subconsciously want to be fulfilled. So, if you die in your dream, maybe you want to die in real life. The fact that this creature has your face could mean suicide. Are you still taking your medications?"

"Yes," Camden lied. The medications messed his perception up, so he had stopped taking them a few months ago after an episode in the shop. No one had gotten hurt, but he'd been so shaken that he refused to take them again. Telling the doctor would have been a waste of time, since he would have disagreed with the choice. Side effects included a psychological numbness. After the depression and fits of rage in the early years, the apathy had been a relief. The medications had brought him from the hole of depression and unlocked the chains of self-loathing. Day after day, he sat on a scale, pinned in place to keep him from teetering. When he had brought up the dullness and disinterest to Morgan, the doctor had said it was good he didn't want to kill himself anymore. So, that was that. Either feel nothing or want to die. Camden didn't see much difference in either, but he took them every day for the entire second half of his pubescent life and through his young-adult one. All these years of rattling that scale, he pulled the pin. Something about knowing something the doctor didn't also brought potential. Morgan poked into his personal life, he prodded at his emotions, and he loved dragging any form of irritation out. Withholding information gave Camden a rush from the one ounce of control he had.

"Good, I would hate to lose my favorite patient," said Morgan.

Camden forced a modest laugh, but it came out unnatural and awkward. He said, "I bet you say that to all your patients." It was likely Morgan was lying, but Camden wasn't sure it was a lie. The government had stopped paying the fees after six months, yet Morgan still kept him on the schedule. The pay Camden could give was less than substantial compared to what the doctor would get from government-appointed patients. Maybe he was just the charity case. There was a rumor that most patients didn't stick around for long. Camden figured Morgan chased them all away. The better question was why Camden kept coming back, knowing what he knew. This wasn't helpful ... except it was.

Camden had been a ball of raw emotions and broken feelings when he first started with Dr. Morgan. After a few months of misery and depression, he saw the real villain. The doctor poked and poked him until he was almost numb to the jabs, until he didn't feel anything. The doctor had taken a soaking-wet towel and squeezed until it dried. It could have been the medications, but despite Camden feeling like he was in a fishbowl, he never dulled that way around Morgan. After accepting therapy, taking the medications, and being hyper-aware of Morgan's sadistic nature, he noticed the subtle details about his doctor. The game they played became fun. Camden hated the man but enjoyed his company.

"Anything happen at work that could have brought this on?" Morgan asked as squeezed the laser pen on and off. Camden's jaw clenched.

"Not particularly," Camden said. *Had anything happened?* Mechatronologists fixed damaged androids, and Camden worked out of a garage below his house in an older part of town. He worked on remolding destroyed parts, reconnecting tubes and wires, and fixing errors in broken codes day in and day out. Although, the doctor asked for particular instances. His memory recalled a moment where a bionic arm had flickered before him. One second the arm had been wires, silicone, and tempered steel; the next it had been a severed human arm bleeding all over the counter. Camden didn't even blink in response to these thoughts.

To him, hallucinating the parts he worked on as actual flesh and blood was a regular occurrence. Those hallucinations weren't even the worst he would see. When he first started work, Camden had torn the garage apart when one android morphed into a kid right before his eyes. The kid had looked at him with curiosity as he tore out its guts. Not even his coworkers could calm him down after that happened. When he had come out of his panic attack and irrational insanity, they had tied him to a support beam, gagged him, and left him alone in the garage. The android, missing half its insides and an arm, had to untie him, since his coworkers left the garage and his employment. When he called them about why they quit, they had told him to get some help. Camden worked alone since. The medications helped with the hallucinations, but now that he'd stopped them, they ran rampant. He figured he'd get used to them. After all, Camden knew what wasn't real.

"Camden." Morgan pulled him back. "Have you been seeing flashes of things that aren't real again?"

"No." Camden lied poorly; the doctor's eyes had to keep themselves from rolling. Morgan ran a hand through his hair, something he never did. He prided himself on looking perfect, so when he forced his hair gel to loosen strands, Camden must be pissing him off. Camden could almost laugh if the subject didn't make his stomach cramp.

"What do you see?"

Morgan's eyes bored into him with an intensity; he loathed when Camden locked up or feigned control of his emotions and despised when Camden lied. Morgan preferred the times when he lost his shit, threw things, and collapsed in a puddle of tears. The doctor would spend months building up that glass of emotions to relish in the overflow. Resigned, he said, "I see human parts, and I sew together bleeding arteries and burn flesh back together."

"How does that make you feel?" Camden knew Morgan didn't give two shits that he hallucinated androids were human. What he wanted resulted in him getting defensive or offended enough to cry. Morgan loved it when he cried, though it had been a while since Camden last lost control in a session. Camden had spent a long time rehearsing in his head different ways to force Morgan's conversations to his advantage, and the benefits brought him ease.

"It doesn't," Camden said. "I feel nothing."

"That would be the medications." The defiance made Camden's heart leap. However, seeing human blood instead of android lubricant bothered him. Every time it happened, the world tilted on its axis and brought a hammering in his gut. After blinking over and over, they would eventually stop so he could continue his work before the next one. Morgan asked, "Are you still going to see Lisa?" Changing subjects often meant that the doctor couldn't draw any more emotion out of the current one, or he was unaware of Camden's withheld information.

"Not lately." Camden's stepmother was senile. The punch to his abdomen never got easier when she called him by his father's name. The man had died a couple years ago, and Camden didn't cope well if any subject pertained to him. Morgan knew to steer clear of that one, lest he get shut out. This was not the reason he avoided his stepmother, though. That could be blamed on the hallucinations again. "I've just been busy with work."

Morgan nodded. "And what about your relationship with Jenna? Are you staying sexually active?"

Right, this question. Avoiding it altogether, he said, "Jenna is great." Morgan waited to watch each of Camden's subtle muscle movements of discomfort. "She wants me to move in with her." He would not answer that second question. He never did.

The doctor leaned back and propped his foot back on his knee. "Are you going to?"

Why did he care? Camden glanced at a mechatronic bird as it flew too close to the window. The bird hovered as it scanned the structural integrity of the glass, then flew off, "I don't know. The garage is just downstairs. I would have to get up early to get to work on time if I did."

"Seems like you have it figured out then," he said, ending that train of conversation.

Time should be almost up now. Camden glanced back at the clock on the wall behind him and saw that only fifteen minutes had passed. Dread coated his face. Didn't Morgan only ask about his sex life at the end of the session? They still had forty-five more minutes. Camden's stomach clenched. As much as Morgan entertained him, spending more time with him did not fare well. Not today. The skit they always played for each other was practiced and exact, but today improvised and unnatural.

"Is something wrong? Do you have something to do later?" Camden turned his face back to Morgan, trying to hide his alarm and failing. The doctor's grin, so blatant, brought a dizziness; he could pass out from embarrassment. The little wins were always monumental, but the losses made death reachable. Camden's heart raced. No. Not another panic attack. "Camden?"

He looked away, anywhere else. No way this could set him off. There was no way he just fell into that trap. Dr. Morgan seemed concerned, but his devilish face grinned. The psychiatrist walked over and put his hands on Camden's shoulders, trying to ground him.

"Are you all right? Talk to me. What's happening?" Morgan sounded so far away. The pounding in his ears deafened him. He couldn't breathe. Camden tried to, but no matter how deep or how much he took in, his lungs dried up. Morgan's thumb pulled his eyelids back, and a light blinded him once, then twice. "Here, drink. Calm down. Take deep breaths." Fingers forced him to take hold of a cup. Water. He tried to sip the water, but his body rejected help. Camden shook. He pulled his knees up on the chair, hugged them, and pressed his face into the top. Morgan's concerned face spun in circles like they were caught in an earthquake. His lips held back a smile, but the crinkled crow's feet gave away all they needed. Clawed fingers held his shoulder. No, no, no. Rocking back and forth, he tried to push away memories. A hand reached up and pulled his head, yanking his face up. Something pressed against his face. "Breathe into this." He complied.

When the attack passed, Camden didn't let go of his legs or the paper bag. Dr. Morgan's hair had several strands out of place. He regarded his patient with careful eyes as he backed up to sit back down. Camden's chest hurt. "Doctor," he mumbled, "what if the creature from my dream had *your* face?" Silence. Camden looked up for a tell, but he still only watched. No tells. He continued, "What if you were the one that caused me terror and ate me?"

"That's preposterous," Morgan dodged. "I'm your friend, Camden. I would never mean to cause you any more pain. I am here to help you."

"Nnngh." Camden's stomach tensed, and he forced the bile back down, rocking back and forth, causing the chair to squeak. "Doctor, I'm afraid."

"Of what, Camden?"

"I don't know." Camden looked back at his doctor, whose sadistic grin pierced his insides and twisted them around. "I think I'm afraid the abyss will swallow me whole."

"The abyss?" he asked, hiding his teeth.

"There is a darkness inside me," Camden began. Why did he talk? He had to keep reminding himself this was therapy. Therapy only worked if he talked about things that bothered him. "It closes around me, and I feel as if it'll take me anytime it wants. I have no control over anything. There's just fear, unrelenting fear all around me. It's suffocating me. Those hands touch me, and they tear through my skin. I thought I had control. I thought I could prevent it from taking me if I just didn't acknowledge it. But it did anyway." Tears glided down Camden's face. "I died, Doctor. I actually died."

"You're not dead, Camden. You're alive. You feel, right? So, you're alive. Hold on to those feelings, and know you can't be dead if you have them."

"But I didn't," Camden said, looking up at his doctor's waiting and confused face. "I felt nothing. I felt like I was dying, and then nothing."

"If you died, how could you even comprehend that you felt nothing? It's just a dream," he said.

"I felt nothing, but I was still aware. I think." Camden loosened his grip on his legs. "But everything was different after I died. It smelled so intensely of my fear. Then there was nothing. And then ... rage. Pure, unbridled anger oozed from all around the darkness. I didn't feel it personally, but it was so severe that I think it brought me back to life." Morgan blinked but never took his eyes from his patient. He froze in his chair. This conversation bothered the doctor, and he could only assume why. But he needed this out of his system, "It's like when you watch a movie and a character you have no connection with has emotions. You can see them clearly, but you don't feel them. But if I wasn't angry, then why did it bring me back to life?"

"It's a dream, Camden," Morgan said, annoyed. He bobbed his leg up and down, losing interest in the conversation, trying to ditch it altogether.

Camden looked up into the doctor's gray, unenthusiastic eyes. "I don't think it was, Doctor. I've never felt anything more real."

"You need to let go of these fantasies," he said. "Dreams are just your mind playing tricks on you. They're entertaining. That's all. Sometimes, feeling something in your dream is the entertainment you need. You didn't die. You're alive and well."

Camden's dark eyes looked deep into the sadistic gray, and he wanted him to hurt. Somehow, some way, he wanted him to feel like a worm whose feelings meant nothing. Just how he made him feel. Camden searched his thoughts and his memories for every detail to find a way to hurt Morgan the way Morgan hurt him, but he hadn't the slightest idea how. He knew the things that annoyed him and what made him smile. Camden needed to see Morgan exhausted more than anything, so he searched for something. Anything ... What did he value? He valued causing others pain. He appreciated causing Camden pain. What if Camden had no pain? Not like the dulling the medication brought on, but something immediate. Camden's eyes flicked to the unopenable wall of windows. Then he stood to look closer at them.

He looked down at the city below. Cars zipped by, people the size of bugs moved like dots, and Camden regarded it all with static emotions. The vertigo spun his eyes, but he didn't shy away from it like normal. Over by Morgan's desk, he dug through the single drawer. Old-fashioned pens that he never used rolled around, and the uncharged holo-tablet slid to the back. Camden approached the bookshelf. Psych books alphabetized neatly throughout the shelves. The leather journals he recognized sat at eye level. He pulled off the red one first and opened.

"Camden, it's not okay for you to look at those." Dr. Morgan strolled over to take it from him, but not before he saw a few comments. The chicken scratch was unexpected. He figured Morgan's handwriting would be elegant and flawless, but the letters came out erratic and sharp. Morgan placed the journal back on the shelf as Camden eyed his doctor's clenched jaw. Turning, Camden yanked the drawer out of his desk, surprising Morgan. All his pens and the tablet scattered onto the pristine floor. "Camden, what are you doing?"

Was that a sense of unease in his voice? Camden turned to the window and smashed the drawer's corner into the hard glass, causing a spider web of cracking. He managed another before Morgan wrestled him for the drawer.

"What is wrong with you?" He didn't raise his voice, but the pitch attested to stress. "Stop."

Morgan was strong, but Camden pulled it free to get another bash in the window, shattering it and taking the drawer out with broken glass. Camden teetered as the wind tried to suck him out and down to his death. Hands grabbed hold of his shirt, pulling him back. Their legs tangled, and Camden landed against the softness of a body, not the hard floor. Morgan let out a grunt as Camden's elbow knocked the wind out of him. Wind howled through the open window, dragging any loose object in a current around the room. Camden stood and looked down at Morgan, who clutched his chest, gasping.

"You can't have me," Camden said, turning toward the window. Was he really going to do this? Camden didn't want to die; he just wanted to make Morgan acknowledge him. After taking a single step, he toppled down as Morgan grabbed hold of his ankles to pull him back, smashing his jaw into the wood.

Camden gripped his mouth as blood erupted like an explosion inside. He coughed, spitting a huge glob of it on the floor, but the amount still flowing threatened to drown him. Morgan grabbed his ankles, dragged him along the floor, creating a line of blood, and stopped at the far wall. Morgan pinned his arms behind his back and sat on him while he called for his secretary. Stars shot through Camden's vision during the whole ordeal. Everything spun, and he couldn't move under the dense weight of his doctor. His chin throbbed, and his mouth was a volcano of agony and blood.

"You can't!" Camden screamed, spraying blood everywhere. "You can't do this!"

Morgan leaned down to whisper in his ear. His hair must've been all over the place, because hairs touched his neck. A shiver ran down his spine as he said the words, "Says who?"

Camden's face thumped into the wood floor as he fainted.

4

Freedom

Camden's ears picked up sound before his body understood the situation. The clicking of heels in the outside hallway grounded him, and he opened his eyes to a plain gray ceiling. He let out a moan when the pain in his mouth came with his return to consciousness and reached up to feel his tongue. But his arms caught on something; they had bound his wrists and limbs to the bed with leather cuffs. They weren't tight, but he doubted he could struggle out. Foggy-eyed, he looked around at the whitewashed hospital room. A heart monitor blinked without sound out of the corner of his eye. How did he end up here? He recalled going to Morgan's appointment, the panic attack, then ... Oh yeah. He had tried to kill himself. Camden sighed. He had lost it.

The source of the heels entered the room: a young android wearing a nurse's tunic. Though they didn't look different from humans, she had not invested in a unique face mold. Androids liked to commission a unique face mold in their early years. Only one of the twenty female factory creations looked that neutral. Camden saw her nametag said Tera, so she had to be at least a year old. Androids rarely picked their names younger than a year old. She crossed her arms over her scrub tunic and smiled before saying, "Good evening, sir. Can I get you anything to eat?" Camden watched as her processing systems scanned him. He returned the favor. Her silicone skin covered a dense collection of steel wiring that twisted up to act as a muscle structure. Though he could not see past her silicone, he knew every detail of her steel frame, tubing, and wires. Specially crafted glass eyes flicked back and forth to each of his brown ones. She spoke again. "You need to eat."

"Where's my psychiatrist?" Camden asked, mouth full of gauze.

"Doctor Morgan has gone home for the day. You'll need to wait until tomorrow to speak with him," she said.

He tugged on the restraints. Although his head still spun, massaging his temples required hands. "Why do I feel so dizzy?"

"We have administered Ativan to help you relax. Also, we tested your blood. You have not been taking your medications as requested. Please follow all the doctor's instructions from now on."

Camden stayed quiet. Had he really planned to jump out the window? What would that have proven? His obsession with hurting Morgan had seemed the best course of action at the time, but retrospectively only proved he needed the medications. Camden didn't want to die, but his mind had gone right to suicide. Tera approached him for a checkup. She worked with gentle hands to bandage the bruise on his chin and change the bloody gauze in his mouth. Her fingers were warm from the circuitry resisting electrical currents. It was a nice touch using the excessive heat to make them more human, but the wires themselves needed to stay cool. He closed his eyes as she moved to fiddle with his IV tube. Though her curt and precise mannerisms made it obvious how young she was, he tried to remember the first time he'd seen a baby android. His brain grew foggy as he recalled a distant memory in his father's workshop. But his thoughts slipped through his fingers as sleep took over.

Morning brought the light through the thin curtains and a tray of breakfast that looked more like mashed crayons. His cuffs pulled on the bar, holding them as he tried to stretch. Out of a sense of frustration, he rattled his bound limbs to exert the pent-up energy. Tera watched with her analytical face, placed the tray down, and fed him from a spoon. Turns out the mushy crayons tasted like fruit. She asked him question after generic question as she watched his vitals. After breakfast, she unbound him before leaving. A proper stretch ensued before he eyed the screenless television, attempting to figure out how to turn on the holograms. Despite his expertise in mechatronics, these televisions confused the daylights out of him. Numbness ebbed away, bringing the beginnings of agony.

"Camden?" A familiar voice broke off his thoughts. Closing his eyes, Camden prepared himself. He turned to see a worried Morgan, catching him off guard. Morgan stepped toward the bed, unsure of every step. "How are you feeling?" The purple under his eyes was uncharacteristic, though his hair and clothes did not mirror the exhaustion in his steps.

"It hurts."

"I'm sorry about that." Morgan dragged the chair to sit close to the bed, never taking his eyes off his patient. "Do you remember what happened?"

"Yeah." Camden looked back at the wall as if his favorite show played holographed there.

"You lied to me," he said. "You said you've been taking your meds."

Camden pursed his lips and didn't reply. What was he going to tell him? That he tired of his life passing by, and he wanted to feel something again? He should have, but he feared that Morgan would say no and dismiss him. "I was so worried that if I let you go, I'd lose you."

Lose him? No, he wouldn't have jumped. It was just a ... scare tactic? Maybe he should be on the medications if that's the course his brain took. Camden really understood nothing about himself. "I don't really know what I was doing."

"I made a mistake. I should have paid more attention to the dream. I'm so sorry. You were trying to tell me you wanted to die, and I just wouldn't see it. I'll try to do better." Morgan hung his head.

"I don't want to die, Doctor," Camden said. "I just want to not be afraid of everything."

"Are you afraid of me?" Morgan looked up at him with such sincere eyes that Camden doubted the sadism. He opened his mouth to lie, closed it, and nodded.

A quiver on the edge of Morgan's lip gave away a foreign emotion. His eyes held more familiar ones. "I'm so sorry. I thought if I disregarded the dreams, you could confirm they weren't real. I'm so stupid."

This new compassionate Morgan was not the one he familiarized himself with, and these unused expressions made it nearly impossible to read him. Was he just playing a game? Was this one of those things that caused Camden to soften, only so he could crack him harder? "Doctor, can I be left alone?"

"Of course." Morgan stood and walked toward the door, then hesitated, "If you need anything, just call Tera." He then left Camden to his thoughts. Was he losing it? Morgan had been so sincere sounding that regret and doubt bubbled all over. Everything made sense when he labeled the psychiatrist a sadist, but what if he was lying to himself so he didn't have to face his own depression?

Jenna came bursting through the door, wearing her still-wet polka-dot raincoat, interrupting his thoughts, and collapsed on his bed, sprinkling droplets all over him. "They told me you tried to kill yourself." She sniffled, making him realize not all the droplets contained fresh rain. Her arms wrapped around his neck as she wept.

His chin stung at the touch, and he hissed. She said, "Oh, my darling, you were doing so well. What happened? Did you have an episode?" Camden nodded. "I should have been there, then—"

"You couldn't have known. They're random, remember?" he said.

"I know, but if I had been there, I could have calmed you down." She pressed her hand to his face, and he closed his eyes, feeling her warmth. Though the touch was similar to Tera's, he felt less surprised and more impressed. Camden didn't want to look at her red eyes and puffy cheeks, but he forced himself. He owed her that. Why hadn't he thought about her? She meant so much to him, but she hadn't been in his mind.

"There was nothing you could have done. Please stop beating yourself up." He didn't like her worrying. He was cruel to her, and now he greatly regretted his actions from the other day.

"I know. I just hate that you're hurting. You don't talk to me about the things that bother you." She cradled his hand in hers and ran a thumb over the top. "Do you know what set it off? Could you talk about it with him?"

Camden flipped his hand up and entwined his fingers in hers. The static from the touch calmed the irrational thoughts fighting his rational ones. "Yeah."

"Will you talk about it with me?" she said immediately, taking it back. "No, wait, I don't want to set you off. It's okay. Just rest."

Camden sighed. "Thank you."

"I love you." She brought his hand up and pressed it to her lips. He smiled a sad smile as he thought about the gap he would have left had he jumped.

Δ Δ Δ

Camden yawned when he woke and immediately flinched as pain ebbed from the wound on his tongue. The dark room told him the time. The lights from the monitors cast an intermittent light around the room. Sleep planned to avoid him tonight.

A voice echoed around him. "Is this what you do with it? I really hoped you'd not waste the life I gave you." His blood ran cold. A figure leaned against the base of the bed. He scurried closer to the headboard and clutched the blanket to his chest. His heart monitor lit up more frequently. "Camden," the stranger said, "I don't want you to give up that which I went out of my way to get for you."

"Who are you?" he asked.

The figure walked closer, though Camden saw nothing extra. The figure was still muted from light. "Who are you?" they said back. The monotone voice, though deep, was not enough to assume they weren't female. "Isn't that why I gave you a second chance? So you can find out who you are?"

"I don't know what you're talking about," he said as the makings of a panic attack rose in his chest. Was he dreaming? This couldn't be real, right?

The figure circled away from the bed to lean against the wall near the door. A gentle contrast between the shape and the white walls allowed him to see the figure cross their arms, "Don't waste my time. Show me who you are. Show me what you are."

Camden shook his head, eyes wide as he tried to get them to focus enough to see better, but the figure didn't reflect enough light to see any identifying features. "That was a dream. This is a dream."

He felt the eye roll, even in the dark. Their emotions came through clear enough, despite not seeing them. His panic withered, and the monitor steadied at a faster-than-resting pace. Camden's skin prickled as waves of confusion flowed over him. "Is that what you believe, or is that what they tell you to believe?" the stranger said. This person seemed dangerous, but he didn't sense cruelty or even malice. In fact, they seemed almost familiar. He squinted, blinked, and widened his eyes, trying every technique to acquire any descriptive features. They felt his straining in the air, and they said, "Careful now, look too closely into the darkness, and it'll start to seem like home." The amusement behind the words didn't bring unease. He couldn't see this person, but Camden felt everything between them. The space seemed to close between the bed and the wall. The fear and surprise lay forgotten in the back of his mind. Warmth, a wave of cold, confusion, and not altogether his own. He had to be dreaming or imagining this out-of-body perspective.

"Are you ..." His face burned. "Me?"

A chuckle. Camden's embarrassment caused his monitor to stutter. He wanted to hide, but he figured nowhere existed where he could hide from this person. "We are different." The sincere answer allowed the burning in his skin to cool.

He needed to ask another question. They waited; his skin prickled in anticipation, not his own. "Why do you want to know who I am?"

A smile, the genuine interest in the air swiveled around him as if the particles floating about acted like synapses reaching from their individual nervous systems. The person pushed off from the wall and approached him. "Isn't that the right question? I guess you better start asking more of those. Now, go to sleep."

His body contorted as exhaustion hit him in an unnatural phenomenon. Camden's body flopped awkwardly as he lost consciousness.

Δ Δ Δ

The morning light blinked in from the window. Jenna slept half on the bed, still holding his hand from the night before. Had she left him during the night? *Was it a dream after all?* He was losing touch with reality, but he cast the episode from his thoughts. He leaned down to kiss her cheek, pulled himself out of the bed, and removed the heart monitors, causing the monitor to flat line; after sliding out his IV, he thumbed a spare cotton ball. Camden shuffled to the bathroom to remove that annoying tube taped to his thigh.

After he came out of the restroom, Tera whispered, so as not to wake his girlfriend. "Dr. Morgan wanted to speak with you when you woke up. He's in the lounge at the end of the hall."

Camden nodded and headed out into the hall after he pulled off the hospital gown and replaced it with scrubs. His T-shirt and jeans existed somewhere, but not here. Down the hall, he passed a handful of empty rooms. He peeked into the lounge to see an unbelievable sight: Dr. Morgan's head pressed against his arms on the table; his back lifted as he breathed. The same clothes from yesterday, now wrinkled against him like he hadn't gone home, while his greasy hair contained old gel. How surreal.

The lounge had three rounded tables, surrounded by several old-fashioned plastic chairs. A buffet bench sat against the far wall, but only a few edibles laid around. Camden placed a hand on the psychiatrist's shoulder and shook him gently. With a shuffle and a yawn, Morgan blinked away the sleep in his eyes and looked at his patient. A small curl at the edge of his lips appeared when he saw who woke him. Morgan brushed his hair back, though it didn't stay. He said, "Did you just wake up?"

"Yeah. What are you doing here? Did you not go home last night?"

Morgan lowered his gaze to the scrubs Camden wore, but they were distant, not really seeing. "No. I uh— had paperwork to fill out. How's Jenna? She didn't leave your side once."

Camden's stomach twisted, though he couldn't figure why. Around the room, his eyes wandered to the cream-colored walls and the unrelated, uninteresting framed holographic paintings. They had fascinated him once, but after he learned the science behind them, he thought them wasteful. The buffet had oranges and bananas laying out, though not fresh. Camden said, "I should take her something. She must be hungry."

Their general friendly conversation brought back old memories of when he hadn't noticed the glint in Morgan's eyes. "Actually, I wanted to talk to you." Morgan leaned back against the molded plastic and fixed the buttons on his vest and gestured for him to sit down. Camden sat across the table from him in an equally unpleasing plastic chair. Magnetized chairs were more comfortable, but it looked like the hospital couldn't afford them. He shuffled around a bit until Morgan brought his attention from his discomfort. "Why did you stop taking your meds? Do you understand how dangerous that is for someone like you?"

"Someone like me," Camden said, looking at a chip on the edge of the table. *Someone crazy.* "Why not just lock me away and be done with it?"

"That wouldn't help you, and it would be a step backwards. You were doing so well before, so why stop?" Morgan asked.

The crack in the table had a little piece hanging off, begging for attention. Fingers twisted at that piece of plastic like a hangnail. "Because I want to feel something again. Anything. For years, I was numb to everything, and now I just want to live a real life. I just go through the motions day to day with no expectations. That's no way to live. Where's the love I'm supposed to feel? Where's the pain?"

"We could have talked about it," Morgan said, "You shouldn't have decided alone."

"You would have said no." The plastic fought against him as Camden's short fingernails tried to get a decent grip but kept slipping away, "You would have shut me out and dismissed me like you always do."

"That's not fair."

"No." Camden stopped tearing at the table and looked up at Morgan's gray eyes. "What's not fair is having to choose between two evils. I either feel nothing and live a decent life or too much but sometimes feel like I want to die. I can't take it anymore. And you," Camden continued, pressing his brows together, "you sit over there with your stupid grin every time I want to scream, like watching me fall apart is your favorite show. I'm coming apart at the seams, and you just laugh at me."

Morgan's eyes narrowed. He laced his fingers together—flashes of talons. Camden blinked—normal, well-kept fingernails. He frowned back at Camden and said, "Camden, I'm not your enemy. Why do you keep making me out to be a villain?"

"Because you enjoy my pain—no, don't you dare deny it." Camden raised his voice as Morgan opened his mouth to interrupt. "I'm done. After I check out of here, I'm canceling our appointments. I won't see you anymore."

Morgan's eyebrows began some dance as his face crinkled and smoothed. It was something Camden hadn't seen before. Morgan's knuckles strained white as he spoke. "I don't think that's a good idea. You need to—"

Camden stood up. "Stop telling me what I need." He slammed his index finger into the table. "I need to live my life. You, those meds, they aren't any way to live."

Camden relaxed his arms to his sides while Morgan's face continued its weird spasming, creating wrinkles. He said, "Please, don't be hasty. You need to reconsider."

Camden sighed and headed toward the lounge door. He stopped next to Morgan and said, "Good-bye, Dr. Morgan." Then he continued.

A clawed hand grabbed his wrist, stopping Camden in his tracks. He jerked his head around in disbelief. Morgan. No claws, just Morgan's hand. "You want to feel?" The voice sounded off, and Camden looked at Morgan's grave resolution. "You want the pain?" That grin returned. "I can make you feel again."

Before Camden made sense of what he'd said, Morgan pulled him forward, rolling him onto the floor back toward his chair. A scuff sounded as the metal legs skittered on the linoleum. Baffled, Camden watched as Morgan stood over him with his familiar face plastered so blatantly. "What?" Camden said.

Morgan descended on him, pressing him hard into the floor, grabbing hold of his scrubs collar and crushing the air from his lungs. Camden tried to tell Morgan to get off, but he didn't have any ammunition. He gasped as Morgan watched in quiet fascination. Morgan ran a clawed finger down his cheek. No. Not claws. "You need me, Camden." Camden shook his head, still choking air into his chest cavity. Morgan leaned down, his eyes lowered, and whispered in Camden's ear, "Well, I need you. I can give you what you want. I can make you feel alive." Tears rolled down Camden's cheeks as the chokes became shaky gulps. He said, "Let me show you."

Morgan's hands pulled down Camden's scrub collar to bite him hard, bringing back the same shocking pain he recognized from the dream. A scream, stifled by the other hand cupping his mouth, tore the healing tissue on his tongue. He thrashed, but neither the hand on his mouth nor the sharp teeth tearing his skin came loose. Through skin, through muscle. He shook and twisted. Camden tossed his body underneath the unnaturally heavy one above him.

His arms lay pinned beneath the man as they clenched and unclenched, trying to force Morgan off. The mouth came free. The psychiatrist leaned back, pressing Camden's face into the floor, and let out a breathy groan. With both hands, Morgan forced Camden to look up at bloody teeth that dripped down at him. Camden opened his mouth to scream for help, but Morgan's thumbs took hold of his now-open mouth and pushed. The scream that came out created a guttural hum. The thumbs dug deeper and pressed into his throat, keeping him silent.

Blood splattered out of his mouth onto Camden's face as he spoke. "Don't you feel so alive?" Camden's tightened eyes didn't focus as he continuously heaved from the thumbs invading his throat. Morgan leaned down to whisper in his ear again, sending an involuntary shiver down his spine. "Shall I take your ear next?"

Teeth raked over his ear, placing a little pressure on the lobe. He sampled the top cartilage and tore a bite free. Choked, gulped gasps bubbled out of Camden's mouth. His entire body shook and kicked and clenched like seizing. Gauze caught fresh blood from his old wound. Morgan spat the piece onto the floor with a wet smack and gave a loud sigh. The spasming slowed, but Camden gripped on to that pain like a lifeline. If he let go, nothing would be left.

5

Gear

This sad world and its sad people ceaselessly tired Gear. Initially he had thought humans were an endless supply of information and that no two were alike, but he found the patterns and social construct limited. Societal expectations created personal interests that narrowed the possible outcomes. Humans just weren't that interesting. Gear analyzed the mannerisms and responses for decades, and what he found exhausted him. They could be so much more, but humans were selfish, and the focus fell on keeping a tight leash on anything that acted or looked different. So here he was, staring into the bright-blue and white swirling liquid containing intoxicants. The world didn't need him, but it liked to think it did.

"R8P1030." It didn't sound like a question. "I have a job for you."

Gear cast a look over to the woman leaning against the bar. His facial-recognition software was down, so she looked like a weird glitch. He wasn't even sure she was human, though he could guess. "Not interested, though I appreciate you bothering to learn my whole serial code."

She didn't move. "I can pay you, monumentally."

Gear puffed out exhaust, closed his eyes to try to focus any of his socialization programs, to no avail. This lady didn't get it, and he couldn't formulate the right words to get her to leave. "Didn't you hear me? I said I'm not interested."

He opened his eyes as she slid a post note over next to his glass. The yellow paper had a single word etched in ink on it. A name. Before she walked from his peripheral view, she said, "If you change your mind."

Gear's eyes didn't leave the note. He wasn't sure they were working anymore. The processes of his thoughts were elsewhere. Humans demanded things; humans always got their way. Who was he to deny their every order? The handwriting was large, used confident strokes, but smudged in places. He finally pulled his eyes from the note back to his drink. The swirls calmly made spirals as the nanobots danced, looking for programs to crash. Gear couldn't understand quite why, but he glanced back to the note. It was gone.

With surprise, he looked around to see if it fell off the bar. The sound of everyone around him came back into focus, and he gripped his head. His auditory program must've been hit by the nanobots and reset itself. The shock of it brought him back to the bustling room filled with androids. Where had that note gone? Gear tapped the counter to signal to the robot behind it. The barkeep, not an android, was a mechatron that had a simple nonadapting AI. The movements were janky and efficient telling of a time prior to the Renaissance. Gear liked that robots didn't understand the need for subtle inefficiencies, and he longed for their naïveté.

"The woman left a note," he said. "Where did it go?"

"There is no woman," it replied.

"She left a moment ago," Gear said but knew the robot either didn't see her or had an error. "The note she left must've fallen behind the counter."

"There is no woman," it said. "There is no note."

Gear waved it off and looked back into his drink. She hadn't been here, but Gear didn't pride himself in having an imagination program. He strictly worked in possibilities and the practice of keeping order. Gear's circuitry buzzed with uncertainty. His programs tried to understand, to reach a conclusion, but he couldn't work through the random systems shutting down on him. Dipping into his memory, he scanned the image of the note. He found a whole lot of corruption, either from the nanobots or some misunderstanding. The woman, though he clearly remembered the interaction, did not leave any hard evidence of her existence. A strange bubbling sensation, not entirely the drink, fluttered in his stomach cavity. A ghost woman and a name on a note gave him a mystery. Gear couldn't help himself. The need to understand got the better of him.

Gear opened a search index. With another tap of his fingers, the barkeep arrived to take payment.

Δ Δ Δ

Gear's home was a loft above a peculiar android occupation venue. He sat in the dark on a couch facing a set of tinted windows. After expunging the nanobots from his system using the conduit attached to the support box, he scanned the name again. It was a person, of that he was sure. Face after face blinked by, adding increments to his interest. Normally, jobs were straightforward and uninteresting. There were always reasons people did things, and Gear made an easy living predicting human actions.

This was different. There was always a story. Yet this one only came with a name. No number, no contact information, no instructions. There wasn't even a last name. Gear's system paused on a government identification document of a man. His system recognized the ink type when the signature was signed. An identical smudge was positioned within the etching of the name. The signatures were identical. This was the target.

"What does she want me to do with you?" Gear said to the brown eyes staring back at him. A weird buzzing sensation filled the back of his head, but he ignored it. "So, Camden, who are you?"

A couple hours passed while Gear logged as much public information into his memory as he could about the man. He couldn't figure out a single reason why anyone would have an interest in him, but he kept digging, hoping for anything out of the ordinary. The only thing going for him was his recent admittance into a psychiatric ward. So, the man had a few screws loose. What did that matter to the job? What even *was* this job? Gear shut down a few programs and let the main one focus. His Sherlock program could solve any mystery, and this one would be no different. Yet, all it seemed to do was run the same numbers over and over and display them. There wasn't enough information to arrive at a conclusion.

Gear huffed and tried a new search. It was interrupted by his roommate barging through the front door of the loft, flicking on the lights and saying, "What are you doing in the dark?"

The mechanical optics narrowed his pupils so he could see, and he looked over the back of the couch at the female android as she sauntered up to him. "Working."

Rave, with her baby-blue, knee-high fuzzy boots and her orange, polyvinyl-chloride dress, looked like a walking toy. In some sense, she was. Her hair, a little past her shoulders, created a rainbow, and her eyes, at the moment, were blue. She leaned over the back of the couch as Gear slowly shuffled toward the edge. "I thought you said you were taking a break."

"It got boring," Gear said as she leaned on her wrist and raised an eyebrow. "Actually, I could use your surveillance access."

She eyed him, then hoisted herself over the back of the couch to land next to Gear. "Sure. Whatcha need?"

Gear sent her time stamps for the psych ward as well as the clinic prior to Camden's admittance. Rave's eyes went vacant as her systems scanned the cameras. Gear waited not so patiently for new information. The camera feeds held data that would add to his understanding of the job and his target. They would show his patterns, and Gear would be able to solve the equation.

Rave's fingers twisted her shimmering rainbow hair, and Gear watched unamused. It was a habit she added to her system to seem more attractive to humans. The more attractive she was, the more clients she had, and the more money she made as a companion android. Gear watched her twist the poor strands of hair and irritate the nanites. Android hair had two variants: either nanites that connected to the circuitry within, allowing them to change the color at will or human hair woven through the silicone. Rave often changed her hair color, so nanites suited her best, while Gear left his woven brown hair the same way it was two decades ago when he had his face mold commissioned. It was the same for their nails. She preferred the nanite nails that she could change, while Gear preferred other add-ons for his fingers.

After about two minutes, Gear asked, "You done? Did you find anything?"

Rave puffed her lips. "Don't be cute."

"I'm not being cute. I'm asking you if you found anything," Gear said which made her chuckle. He didn't know why she laughed, and he really wished she'd either directly send him her feed or tell him what she saw. Another few minutes ticked by, and the only way he could force himself to be patient was to count the seconds.

Finally, she crossed her legs and leaned back. "Interesting case you got here. I suppose you'll tell me what's important about this guy?"

Not wanting to waste precious moments by explaining to her about the note, he said, "What did you see?"

"Well," she started, "he's not at the psychiatric ward. In fact, I'd say he's been missing for two weeks."

"What?" Gear asked, waiting for her to say more. "How do you know? Where's his last known location?"

Rave narrowed her eyes. "What's got you so riled up? First you wanted to take a break, and now you're practically foaming at the mouth for this job."

"Don't be ridiculous. I don't foam," Gear said. "I'll tell you everything if you just tell me what you have."

She propped her fuzzy boots up on his lap and lay back lengthwise on the couch. With a snarky grin, she put her hands behind her head. "Well, he started in a private clinic, but there's some corruption with the footage. I watched all the cameras around the clinic, but I didn't see any ambulance transfer him to the ward. I did, however, see your man being loaded into the back seat of a car. That's the last eyes I have on him."

"Make and model?" Gear asked, already pulling up the database. She linked to him a still frame of the car, and he analyzed the shape. The car belonged to Camden's psychiatrist, Dr. Morgan. With slight disappointment, Gear downloaded and saved all information on the doctor. He found his address. "Check these locations next."

Gear waited, a little more patiently this time. His program was telling him it was a classic case of kidnapping, and he was overcome with newfound boredom. He stared across at the window as the time went by. It reflected his neutral demeanor, decorated with scrappy brown hair, brown eyes, and an off-center nose plastered on a small male android frame. The female android on the couch next to him was everything he wasn't. Rave wore colors, had flamboyant features, and had a larger, female-shaped android body. She stood as tall as five feet nine inches, while his frame only let him stand at five feet six inches.

Something about his reflection ticked a box in his head, but he wasn't sure which one. He really wished Rave would hurry. His waning interest in the case wasn't mirrored in his need to know the missing answers. The man's name kept repeating in his head as he logged any abnormalities in the man's information. His government identification picture stared back blankly. The brown hair, sunken brown eyes, crooked nose, and short beard all filed into his recognition program. Camden. Camden. Cam.

6

Desire

Camden lay drugged into a stupor on the basement floor. Morgan kept his hands bound all the same. The original use of the small basement room was for storage, but he'd not used it until now. The piping on the wall led into the floor next to a handleless bucket. Camden's scrub shirt was torn, bloody, and smelled, while the scrub pants were becoming ribbons near his feet. Morgan looked at the dried bloodstain on the floor. It was mixed in with the dust underneath the heavy bandage wrapped around Camden's left foot.

Four days ago, Morgan had finally found a use for his tool shed out back. He never used the lawn care other than to mow the lawn, but the unused rose clippers finally had something to clip. Morgan knelt to check the wound he made. With care, he unwrapped the soaked gauze wrapping to find Camden's foot hadn't healed much at all. The bones of his two smaller toes still showed under the adaptic layer. As he changed out the different layers of wound care on his toes, he recalled removing them in the first place.

It had been a spur-of-the-moment decision after a sleepless night. Camden had been getting too rowdy with his escape attempts. Somehow, after a week, he had worked the hinges off the door and made it up to the second door to the basement while Morgan worked. After opening the door, Camden caught him off guard and shoved him to the ground. He didn't make it far, because Morgan kept sedatives near the door in a box. Camden was dragged back to the basement and the door reinforced to prevent further escapes. One weak link in the chain had been wedged between the piping on the wall. After that situation, he manacled his hands behind his back rather than chains on his ankle.

For hours, he debated breaking his legs, and he planned to, but he found the clippers in the shed while looking for a bat or hammer. He still would break his legs, but Morgan really wanted to use these clippers. The next day, after the sedative wore off, he indulged. Taking the thrashing man by his foot, he angled the clippers around his little toe and squeezed the tool's handles. All his toes spread, all his muscles spasmed, and he screamed so loud, Morgan was sure they would both go deaf. Still, the toe didn't cut easily. It took another snip, another, and some twisting to get it free. By then, Camden was sobbing, and blood dribbled from his mouth from the wound on his tongue reopening.

Morgan pocketed the toe in his overalls' pocket. The overalls he put on whenever he visited Camden since he never knew how much blood he would spill. And he ran a finger along the top of Camden's spasming foot, leaving a trail of blood. As he looked at the now-dulled clipper blades, he thought about how a bone saw would have worked a whole lot better. Then, he tore at the second toe.

He held the toes in his hand like prayer beads, running his thumb over them. Camden's drugged eyes stared blankly at the ceiling. Behind him, out of sight, his fingers were missing their nails. Morgan finished his first aid on the foot and rolled Camden face down to see his patched fingers. Unlocking the manacles with his fingerprint, Morgan let his fingers graze the palms as he imagined prying the coarse skin from muscle. Camden's limp body didn't react to the pulling off of bandages or to the application of antibiotic cream. The wounds on each fingertip were not substantial, but they would bother him for months. Two of the wounds had a little infection building up underneath. He tore the healing flesh off to let it drain, then applied the cream before rebandaging them and replacing the cuffs.

Morgan had taken a nail a day for ten days. He ran out of finger-nails the day before Camden's escape attempt. Three days ago, when he brought newly purchased clippers down, Camden began to self-destruct. He screamed and begged, all music to Morgan's ears, then began bashing his head into the solid floor. Two hard thunks had Morgan to him, cradling his head to prevent more. He had shushed him, ran fingers through his hair, and rocked him, but Camden was a wild animal. Morgan hated having to sedate him, but he did, and watched his almost peaceful sleep for a long time. That peacefulness was like falling into a frozen lake. He purchased the heavier drugs that wouldn't render him unconscious after that.

Camden's scrubs were becoming too stiff to move him around easily, so Morgan tore them free to burn. He had picked up fresh ones from the office to change him into but became captivated by the tattoo that ran along Camden's upper arm and down his chest. Crouching down, Morgan ran his fingers along the black circuitry painted into his skin. Not only did he not know Camden had tat-toos, but he had not told him a lot of things. Morgan's fingers dug into the circuits as his nails attempted to break skin. Camden rarely told him anything. Blood rose up when the nails broke through.

These black markings were homage to the machines Camden worked on. The machines, with their false emotions and inability to feel, meant more to Camden than Morgan did. A black square, painted under his skin above his heart, acted as an entrance for the wires that scattered over his back and bicep. Morgan's nails, though short and clean, drew blood from the ink. He wanted to tear it off.

A graft. Yes, he could graft them away. Morgan's clinic didn't have a skin graft on-site, but he could request one from the local hospital. With each chunk of flesh he removed, he could have more of him. As Morgan pranced up the steps from the basement to call in the order, he debated whether he would try the flesh. He didn't want to keep memorabilia of those markings, and wasting precious pieces of Camden didn't settle well with Morgan.

He ran his fingers over the charms on his keychain. The toes were dried, dead, and soft, as if they were still part of Camden. He made a quick call to Tera to have the graft at the office tomorrow. Morgan watched the open door to his basement as the android confirmed his request and hung up. The doorway, dark and ominous, called to him. Down the steps, Morgan descended to find Camden upright on his knees, wobbling to and fro.

With arms clasped behind him, he couldn't even steady himself. The drugs made it impossible for him to get any further. Camden's dulled eyes watched the floor as if they weren't being used. Morgan grinned and leaned against the doorframe. Camden raised his head slowly like a baby deer and looked at his psychiatrist. Morgan wasn't sure he recognized him.

"What big eyes you have." Camden dribbled the line to an old folk tale.

Morgan watched with amusement. "The better to see you with."

Camden rocked a little too far and fell flat on his face without a single grunt. The back of his head was powdered in the light-brown dirt from the floor. Morgan walked over and lifted him back up. His head remained flopped but slowly returned back upright and looked back at Morgan. The darkened eyes were a bit crossed and focused on the lower half of Morgan's face. "What big teeth you have."

Morgan felt a shudder run down his spine and a sharp sensation in his jaw. After wetting his lips, he opened his mouth to say the rest of the line, but the words wouldn't come. If he said them, he wasn't sure he could control himself anymore. And he would not lose it. Not around Camden. He couldn't afford any accidents. As if the wait exhausted him, Camden's head fell backward and hung off his shoulders. Morgan lowered him back to the floor and positioned his head in a less-damaging position. Camden's body was limp, and his eyes were closed. Morgan pressed a hand against his throat to feel the faint pulse. "Don't tempt me."

Camden's neck, so fragile, laid like an offering in his unconscious state. Morgan knew he could crush his bones. It would crunch and crackle like opening a snack from its package. The windpipe would press closed under his grip, and Camden would die quietly without struggle. Nausea and dizziness enveloped Morgan as his fingers wrapped around Camden's neck. There existed nothing else in the world he wanted right that second. But not Camden. Morgan pulled his hand away, leaving not even a red mark. Fingers bent to keep contact, short nails trying to hook in.

Morgan fled the basement, locking each door as he went. With a pounding heart and uneasy breathing, he poured himself a drink. Alcohol would dull the need. The basement could be forgotten if he just drowned in the numbness. Tomorrow, he could distract himself with the skin graft.

7

Rescue

A long time ago, when Dr. Morgan's house was built, it looked high-tech with all those angles, but now it just stood as a relic to a past obsessed with the future. Gear watched it from his vehicle, waiting for more information to come available. The programs within grew idle as he focused on his work. But with the absence of new data, his systems wandered to unnecessary thoughts.

Camden's data kept surfacing as if there was something his scans missed. The man was generic, with no standout features, but something, *something* just kept drawing his focus. Of course, it was ridiculous to fixate on impossibilities, but the system of carbon-fiber muscling went rigid in his hand. Tapping his fingers, he kept count of how many times his process flicked back to the stranger.

"Anything happen yet?" Rave said as she sat upright on the backseat floor.

Gear's entire system flickered, and he made sure the systems didn't corrupt. His eyes didn't leave the house, but he unclenched his hands from the fresh vise grip he held on his knee. "What are you doing in the back seat?"

She climbed into the front seat and fixed her eccentric clothes to line up, despite not being made for anyone to sit down in. "I figured you wouldn't let me come. Especially considering how much this case is bugging you."

"I deal with a lot of weird situations, but they're always explainable. This one is no different," Gear said.

She hummed in hesitance. "Then why are we outside some guy's house in the middle of the night?"

"Surveillance, Rave. We can't all have illegal software." Gear saw movement in the window and zoomed his optics a bit. The doctor, wearing some kind of plastic painter's overalls, came into view through the window he watched. After Dr. Morgan placed a trinket on the kitchen counter, he ran his hand through his hair. With indignance, he poured a glass of whiskey and drank it all in one gulp.

"Wonder what's got him all flustered," Rave said with lacking enthusiasm.

Gear didn't reply right away; he was too busy trying to get a better look at the object on the counter. Something was not filing right, and his scanners couldn't pick up a listing on the product. So that trinket was handmade, but that wasn't quite what had him intrigued. The charms on the chain sort of looked like ...

"Are those toes?" Rave said, reaching the same conclusion. Her recognition software was better in every way, with faces and objects. "Think they're real?" she said with nothing more than curiosity in her tone.

Gear narrowed his eyes to shutter his lens, attempting to zoom in further than his hardware. It didn't work. His Sherlock program ran the odds of those being real since the target's kidnapping. "Possibly," he said.

The man placed the glass on the counter and took the charm into his hand, cradling it. He lifted it to his face, and Rave's nails scraped the dashboard. "Gear." Her voice was curt and serious. After tearing his eyes from the man in the house, he looked at her face. Her eyes were wide and flicked slightly as she zoomed and unzoomed. "He has a lot of first-aid products lying about. Some are used wrappings."

Gear let out some exhaust as his calculations reached their conclusions. "He's in there. The target."

"Alive?" Her eyes returned to normal focus and looked at Gear. He nodded. "Why?" she asked, and he shrugged.

"I don't know that yet, but there is a high probability this Morgan isn't as angelic as all his paperwork makes him out to be."

"Well, you need to save him." Rave's focus turned back to the man in the house for more information or to fuel her sudden appearance of anger. Gear didn't need to look again; he had all the information he needed. Now, it came down to a decision on his part. Technically, he hadn't taken the job, and *technically*, there was nothing he was supposed to do with the target. "Oh, don't you give me that analysis crap. That woman doesn't want him dead, or she would have called someone else."

The disapproval on her face was blatant, but he didn't factor her opinion in. Just her logic. She was right, but he really didn't care much. Humans killing humans was a normal day, so why did this one matter in the grand scheme of things?

"Because you can do something about it. So, do something about it." Rave glared, and Gear narrowed his eyes at her.

"Are you invading my thoughts?" He knew she had illegal programs, but surely this was out of her sense of morality.

"No." She looked away, crossed her arms, and puffed her cheeks. "I just know how that stupid head of yours runs itself."

"You're right," Gear stated, "and though it's not illegal for me to do so, it's unheard of."

"Well, while you decide, take me home." He assumed she was mad. Her tone of voice was at a low frequency, and she wouldn't look at him. "I need to work."

After a few minutes on the road, he asked, "Why are you so set on this?"

She didn't answer, and Gear looked for any sign of movement in her body. Her face was hidden behind her rainbow hair as she looked out the window away from him. Hands rubbed each other in a form of comfort, but Gear figured it was a program she learned by accident. Androids didn't need comfort.

Δ Δ Δ

Doctor Morgan took his car to work around eight in the morning. As soon as it went out of sight, Gear stepped out of his vehicle in full electrical-maintenance attire. It was a favorite of his disguises besides locksmith and pizza delivery. After a quick scan of the neighborhood, he slipped into the backyard. Gear approached the sliding-glass back door and pressed a finger to the electronic lock. With precision, he disabled the alarm and unlocked it.

The doctor's house was decorated in minimalist style, and Gear scanned for anything that could be out of place. It was very quiet. On the counter lay scattered many bandages and antibiotic creams. Around the house, nothing seemed irregular except for a hook near a hallway closet. Gear approached the garment neatly hanging. The plastic overall on the hook was spotless, but the doorknob had residue of dried blood. Gear tried the knob, but it was locked.

He twisted his little finger, and the silicone folded back to reveal access to a tool. After unfolding it, he pressed it into the lock. With a few exact movements, he pushed the door open and folded the tool away. Stairs led down into the darkness of a basement. The foundation was concrete and unfurnished. The first step was too far down, creating a disconnect from the house behind. Gear blinked on his night vision and proceeded.

Another door. This one was latched closed and locked with a padlock like a shed. Two locks for one room. Gear picked the lock and pulled the padlock free. In the dark room, a man lay in the center of the floor on his side with his hands manacled behind him, wearing a set of splotchy scrubs.

Gear stood over him as he confirmed the identity. This was Camden—well, most of him. Bandages wrapped around his feet, his head, and his hands had Gear wondering what other pieces the doctor had removed from him. With a wave of his hand, he overrode the locking system in the cuffs.

The man didn't move, and Gear let out a huff. The small android pulled the larger human up and teetered as his control system accounted for the new center of mass. He carried him up the stairs toward the back door, then out and across the street. Once he placed the man in the vehicle, he tried to compute what to do next. Gear could take him to the hospital, and he turned the vehicle on to drive him there. A call rang in his head, and he picked up to hear Rave's voice. "Bring him home."

Gear spoke internally to her as his eyes flicked up to a camera on the nearest streetlight. "He's not a pet. I'm taking him to the hospital."

"No." It was an order, but then she started to explain why. "The doctor took him from a hospital, remember? We can take care of any emergencies."

"We?"

"I," she said through gritted teeth, but she misinterpreted what he meant. "He'll be safer with us. At least until you can contact that woman from the bar."

Gear let out exhaust, then glanced at the man unconscious in the passenger seat. His scrubs weren't made to look splotchy. The light-blue color was covered in dried blood. "Okay," he said before he even had time to process the information.

Rave hung up after saying, "You won't regret this. You'll see he's safest with us."

Gear watched the road as he decided he already disapproved of the decision. Their loft wasn't equipped properly to house a human. Sure, they had a bathroom and kitchen, but the plumbing didn't work, and all the appliances weren't plugged in. Gear logged all the things that needed to be done in a list and sent it to Rave. The other biggest issue was that Gear wasn't personally equipped to deal with humans. Yes, he understood their behaviors and habits, but that didn't mean he wanted to be around them. Rave, for some reason, put herself in their company often. Working in the profession she did, he wondered why she would want to. With a glance at the human, his system blinked in recognition. *Huh?* Gear ran the facial recognition on the man, but it came back inconclusive. The android narrowed his eyes and decided something must be malfunctioning.

△ △ △

Gear carried the human up the wrought-iron stairs to the loft, through the concrete walls of the main room to the only bedroom in the house: Rave's room. Her rainbow assortment of plastic and fabric laid around in pure chaos. The bed, an untouched decorative piece of furniture, was a gift from a romantic client of hers. Gear deposited him on the red-cushioned surface and walked away toward the main room, where his couch rested. He paused at the door to look back at the human, and a hiding program hissed a shiver of a memory. Gear shook his head to see if some of the cords would rock back in place. Something was not working.

Rave shoved him aside and ran to the human in her bed. She tapped him on the wrist with a nail and scanned the drop of blood. Her eyes, now green, flicked back to Gear as she finished running the blood tests. "He's been drugged."

"Yes." Gear determined that when he didn't react to being moved from the basement. A few seconds passed with blank stares exchanged as they individually calculated what needed to be done.

"He's likely going to have withdrawals," she said, and Gear blinked as a response. "And he's very dehydrated."

"I'll order saline, but it won't get here for an hour. What about work?" Gear said as he put through the order at the nearest hospital.

Rave closed her eyes and expanded her chest cavity to make her look like she breathed deeply. "Right. Well, I'm going to check these wounds now before I go."

She unraveled the bandage on his ear, and they saw the bite shape. Rave paused but didn't verbally acknowledge it. Although Gear found himself trying to match the shapes to the doctor's dental records, he couldn't keep the system from fixating on it when he brought the fresh bandage over and handed it to her. He needed to leave, and he turned to go. Hovering around held no appeal. "I'll be at the bar if you need me."

"Gear." He looked back at her as she called his name. "Thank you."

"For what?"

She shook her head and continued rewrapping his hands. With a tilt of his head, he tried to get a better look at her soft smile, but he wasn't sure he would ever understand her. The programs she had worked so differently from his, and he couldn't fathom what she processed. He left.

The bar was mostly empty at midday. The robot stood idle behind the counter and didn't even respond when Gear sat down. While he waited for the barkeep to power on, he ran diagnostics. Everything came back in great condition, and he tapped the counter. The robot walked over too slowly. The glass didn't fill quick enough, and he couldn't drink fast enough. Gear didn't know the human. Something had to be broken.

The facts were, the man was a mechatronologist. He worked in a small garage. A flicker of recognition. The system clicked off as the nanobots targeted it. He started over. Camden is a mechatronologist. He works in a—

A voice broke his count. "I see you retrieved the asset."

"And how could you see that without doing something illegal?" Gear tilted his head at the woman. Her features were blurred out, and parts of his sight glitched. His optics weren't down, so he restarted the facial-recognition software. It corrupted. *Huh.*

"I must ask," she started, "what made you take the job?"

All of Gear's systems paused. He stared blankly at the woman he couldn't see. "A job is a job."

She rested her arm against the bar. "The human, you know, is in danger." Gear waited for her to finish. "The job is to keep him out of said danger for the time being."

"I'm an investigator, not a babysitter."

"A job is a job," she repeated his own words back to him as she headed toward the exit, leaving him to fume. She paused and said, "And R8P1030, do watch yourself."

After she left, he spent a good few minutes debating how to get Rave to let him take the human to the hospital and dump him. The initial irritation wore off, and Gear sat staring into the swirling liquid, realizing how irrational he was being. He thought back to the bite taken out of Camden's ear and let his programs do their work. They screamed in all fibers of his being, telling him something he refused to listen to. The glass spun as he twisted it. The liquid within was his only solace.

8

Syntax Error

The mind-numbing pain brought Camden back from a nightmare. He didn't expect to want back into the fever dreams until he felt the intensity of his wounds. His fingers thumped agonizingly as the blood pumped against the skin around his missing nails. The chunk out of his ear and missing toes were nothing compared to the screaming headache and nausea that came to life. His mouth released a groan, hoping the pain would cease. It didn't.

Around him, the world glowed red from an antique fabric lampshade. The walls were also red, as was the eccentric heart-shaped bed on which he lay. He twisted his head against the soft pillow. The dusty ground no longer held him captive. Where was he? After an attempt to sit upright, he collapsed back against the bedsheets, but not without seeing the room as a trashcan of neon colors, edgy spikes, and fishnets. Camden's brain couldn't answer any questions, so he didn't ask any. No shackles held him to this room, and the bed was way softer than the basement floor. Though, he wished everything didn't hurt. Whatever drugs Morgan had given him had let him escape, if only for a time. This could easily be mistaken for a dream, if he wasn't acutely aware of every nerve in his body crying for attention.

Camden's body lit a fire within, and he thrashed out of the entanglement of blankets. The room's cool air iced the sweat on his skin, making him regret the action. Grabbing the blanket, he held it close, then threw it away again when he couldn't stand the heat. He wanted to scream. A voice followed a person entering the room. "Here, drink."

Camden looked at the face of the monster from his nightmare. His heart caught in his chest, but then his eyes focused. The android's brown eyes pierced through him as concerned, but the face never changed from neutrality. He held water out to Camden. Shaking, Camden reached for it, but he couldn't hold it. Hands steadied him upright and helped him drink. Cold water rushed in around the wound in his mouth. He flinched but kept drinking. After the glass pulled away empty, Camden asked, "Who are you?"

"Gear," he said. That's all. He said nothing more. The android laid him back down in stoic silence and left the room. Camden shook, thrashing about in the blankets and gripped the sheets but let go instantly as the pain blossomed from his fingers. The android returned and placed a damp cloth to his skin. Camden focused on his ragged panting as Gear wiped the sweat away from his face and neck to cool him down.

This is one of Morgan's plans. Camden was positive. He shoved the android away, who did not indicate surprise. "Stay away," he cried. Gear watched as Camden rolled from the bed with a thump and crawled on his elbows toward the door. The android watched with disinterest yet with an air of concern. He placed the cloth on the nightstand and approached to help Camden up. Camden tugged at the door, pulled it back, and crawled out into a room devoid of furniture and color. He hesitated but felt the android grab him by the stomach. "No!" Camden thrashed as the android dragged him to his feet. Once standing, he shoved Gear away again; Gear's eye twitched in frustration, and Camden hobbled three steps before collapsing. "Argh," Camden grumbled as all his joints reminded him they didn't like his protests.

"Are you done?" Gear said as he leaned against the doorframe with his arms crossed. His neutral face was twisted by something Camden couldn't understand. The creased eyebrows and pursed lips did not exist on the android's face, but they existed somehow. "You can leave if you want, but we've been hired to protect you."

Camden pushed off the floor and rolled into a sitting position to face the android. This was a scheme. Morgan was building up his confidence and safety just so he could rip it apart all over again. He shook violently and eyed the android standing in the doorframe as he regarded Camden with a stony expression. He wouldn't trust this. Let him relearn a comfortable life, then tear it from him. Yeah, that was the plan. Make him think he's safe, then break more pieces off of him. A door opened behind Camden, but he had no strength to change his position. His fingers reminded him by drumming his pulse against the bandages.

"He's awake," the android said. "You want to clean them now?"

Some shuffling, and steps pounded toward him. "Yeah." The owner of a high-pitched voice came into view and crouched down in front of him. Big green eyes blinked at him. She tucked rainbow hair out of her face with a tie. "Hello, there. My name's Rave. I need to check your wounds. Is that okay?"

Camden looked at her gentle demeanor; her smiling face reflected calm warmth. Everything on her face mirrored the strange hallucinations of her false face. She hid nothing except the depth of her heart. His pulse slowed as he recognized what she was. Sliding down to his elbows, then to his back, he closed his eyes, exhausted but not tired.

Her hands wrapped around him, and a current of magnetic energy pulsed into him as she rocked him. A few hushes came from her lips. "There, there. Rave's gotcha." After a few more minutes, she asked, "Can you eat for me?"

Camden opened his eyes. His nausea swam through him as he shook his head. Her eyes and hair shimmered the longer he watched. Nanites. One of her hands ran through his hair. This electromagnetic energy she emitted said one thing, but her choice in clothing said another. He decided he didn't care. The floor fell away as those soft arms carried him back to the bed. The pillow brought pain at the touch. But Rave never left him. Her energy made everything bearable, barely. After several quiet minutes like this, he was sent back into that repeating nightmare to fend for himself.

Δ Δ Δ

Gear watched Rave as she held the human. Electric frequencies flooded out from her in a pulsing wave. He knew them well, but not in this way. This one was a frequency for comfort. Gear watched with newfound interest. Her face was gentle. It was unlike anything he'd ever seen from her. Normally, she carried a degree of sexuality that made her seem out of place, but this ...

"You aren't a companion." He said as it came to him.

Rave glanced at Gear as she checked Camden's wounds. The man didn't stir much. "Are you going to stand there, or are you going to help me?"

Gear crouched and with precision and efficiency, unraveled his foot bandage and cleaned the wound before rewrapping it. Rave noted the ear wound no longer needed bandages and just dabbed it with ointment.

Gear stood upright and stared toward the exit. In situations like this, he normally left, but his curiosity kept drawing him back to his roommate. She was not what he thought she was, and he wanted to know why. But it was not his place. He would not ask. He should leave.

"Hey," she called to him softly, "just because we're made for something doesn't mean it's what we want to do. It's okay to want."

Gear didn't turn around. He couldn't look at the meaning behind her expressions, even if they were just simple programs. The way she said it hadn't been directed about her, and his system grew broiling hot. After a quick check at his coolant levels, his thoughts glorified images of intoxications. Gear said, "I don't want anything. I'm an android."

"Right," she said.

"Can you send me the open feed to that camera outside the doctor's house?" Gear changed subjects as he noticed the time. It was late in the day and time for the psychiatrist to return home from a long day of work to his basement entertainment. Gear wanted to see his reaction to Camden's escape.

Rave didn't respond verbally, but his main process was overridden by an invasive program. Although it was illegal, it was only half so, since he gave her permission. The feed was subpar, but he could make out movement in the kitchen. It took a good fifteen minutes before the doctor went to his basement, paced impatiently back upstairs, made a call, and decided to redecorate. Furniture was thrown, kitchen articles were shattered, and pictures on the walls were torn free. There was something primal and inhuman about it, but the enragement was anything but unnatural. Gear could almost smile if he didn't have to do it voluntarily.

He clicked off the camera feed and looked back at Rave as she held the comatose human in her hands. Camden looked a lot more restful than he had prior to waking in a new atmosphere. Rave's orange eyes watched Gear closely. Gear looked away. "You're good with them." Then he clarified, "Humans."

"And now you know why." She smirked. "I love them."

Androids couldn't love. She was programmed to say and believe that. Then ... didn't that mean Gear was programmed to despise them? No, he didn't hate humans. He couldn't hate.

"I'm a caretaker. I raised kids." She looked back at Camden when he twitched away from something he dreamed. "Children are special." She lifted Camden up and carried him back to the bed to allow him softer comfort than the floor. Then her piercing eyes looked back at Gear. "They absorb everything, and they believe everything has a meaning and is logical. It was my job to show them the joys in meaningless things. And, well, make sure they didn't starve and went to school every day."

Gear didn't understand what she was saying, and his sensors kept coming back with unexplainable results. Little shocks administered in different wires, and he couldn't find any error when the diagnostics report returned. Nothing seemed to be running properly, and he couldn't find the syntax error. "If you liked what you did, why did you become a ..."

"Prostitute?" She lowered her eyes as if recalling a memory. "Sometimes what you are is not what they need. And it's their lives that are more important. Human children differ from children androids, but you love them all the same."

"Androids are never children," Gear stated, and she smirked.

"Is that so?" The silicone creased around her mouth. "And to answer your question, I left my job because I wanted to experience something more. I spent my entire life cycle focused on someone else, so I needed something for me, and this job brought me something completely new. It's not just children that I can help, and it's pretty self-satisfying. Don't we all need our vices?"

"We're made to make their lives better," Gear said as he glanced at Camden. That indicator he couldn't find lit up. He ignored it. *And what do they do for us?* "So, we are programmed to be more human, despite having nothing that comes with being human."

"Are you sure about that?" Rave sat on the bed and gestured to Gear. "Come lay down." Her seductive face promised him a long, drawn-out conversation. They would speak of her past. They would speak of his. He turned away.

With a final look, he saw her lie back to provide comfort for the human. He needed to tell her why he was leaving, so she didn't assume anything. "I have to do some in-depth calculations on this psychiatrist. Maybe he left a trail."

Rave sent him a look with one eyebrow raised. Her eyes seemed to finish a calculation Gear hadn't yet begun. He fled the room too fast. The couch sat waiting, and he waited there until Rave decided Camden could be left alone. She sat next to him. "No viruses tonight? I despise those things, though I guess for you, you'd rather dull all your senses?"

Gear looked up at his reflection, bringing unease. He still couldn't figure out that nagging program that ran when he looked at the human. It buzzed again when he saw his own face. "I don't like the memory files. I'd rather delete them."

"Why don't you?" She asked, but he didn't answer. Rave sat up and scooted into his lap, wrapping her arms around him. "You don't have to tell me, and I won't dig. I'm here. I'll take care of you whenever you need me."

She didn't shock him, and she didn't take any information. He didn't understand the purpose of the touch she gave him. All Gear knew was that he preferred this to all her other affection. The memories flashed in his forward programs, and he cringed. *No, not these.* He shoved them down, but they kept playing. All the processes took a back seat to the recorded memories. They seemed to multiply and play over and over. Was it a virus? Probably. He couldn't delete them either way.

Δ Δ Δ

Gear wasn't a year old, and he had no chosen name. A fresh model made for peak enjoyment instated in the pleasure house where he sat. There was a bed in every room for comfort of humans and a support box in the corner for simple fixes. He hadn't worked too long, and he was still figuring out the irregularities of humans. Gear was too new to know anything of himself; all he understood was that he needed to know more. Each human came in and had their way, or they asked for certain things. He logged each thing and tried to find patterns. There were some, but each human's needs deviated slightly or erratically.

Humans were strange beings. They were all different in their own ways, but they had similarities that brought Gear more confusion. For a while, he and the female model of the same release brought in the most revenue. Despite having many opportunities to learn, it was too narrow, too biased of a category to learn what he needed. After a year, a newer model brought in more money than he did. Gear wasn't special anymore, which he didn't mind so much, but the lack of work brought on boredom.

It was a slow day when they came into his room. It wasn't weird that there were several of them. Humans surprised him, but it was weird that he was the only android. The ringleader was forceful from the get-go. That was typical. He grabbed Gear's chin. "Man, they really make these things perfectly, don't they?" He twisted Gear's neck from side to side, straining the silicone. Then he reached a hand behind Gear's head to lift the silicone on his skull a bit. Gear was unsure of the etiquette for this. He removed a drive, causing half of Gear's programs to freeze. "That should keep things down low. Now for the fun."

Gear looked from side to side as they descended on him. He was built small; until then he hadn't really understood how small. The humans held his limbs as the ringleader plugged a cord into his collarbone port. Gear tested how hard they held him but determined the force of their combined weights was above his ability to lift. The device plugged in blinked to life in Gear's programs. Invasive program. Illegal actions. Gear was being hacked! Facial recognition was hijacked, as was any way he could contact another android. Gear struggled to force any of them off balance. He wouldn't hurt them; he just wanted them off. "This is against protocol. This is illegal," he tried to tell them.

"Aw, look at it," one of them said.

The others laughed, and the ringleader overwrote a program. The coolant tubes flowing throughout Gear's body grew warm. "Stop! This is dangerous."

"For you, maybe." His circuits burned through, and it caused critical errors to pop up on everything. Everything shut down. Nothing was responding. His cooling system couldn't keep up. When they had entertained their human fantasies, he could hear distorted laughing.

"I think we broke it."

"Who cares? This is what they're made for." He got an indicator in his control systems that he had been pushed over.

"Think we'll get charged for breaking it?" another joked.

Gear's auditory program shut down. There was rattling, and the lack of coolant burned out circuits. He would catch fire. He just remembered thinking, *So this is how it feels to die ... Huh.*

Then some of his programs blinked back online. A face, a human. *No more ...* "Man, look what they've done to you. I'll get you fixed up in no time." The human smiled as he pulled him apart and discarded the fried circuitry. The man rewired new wires, cleaned carbon off pipes, and melted the new silicone in place. Gear was sure it took weeks, but to him no time passed. "Try sitting up," the man said as he helped Gear upright. "There we go."

A face watched from the doorway to the garage. It was a child. Gear's facial recognition was off, so he ran no programs. The man checked his work, plugged in a conduit, and started fiddling with processes. Gear watched as the main programs started up the nonessential, surface processes. The kid crawled on its knees into the room to hide under a workbench. It never took its eyes from Gear, and Gear didn't look away from the kid. He had never seen one before. They were so small.

"Cam, come here," the man said. "Let me show you something." The kid crawled out from under the table, and his father picked him up to look at the screen. "You see, this is how they work. And this here is his camera feed on you. They run just like us, but everything they do can be explained through our written languages."

"Can we not do that too?"

"Well, sure, but we don't know the language our processes are written in."

"I don't get it."

"You will one day," he said, bringing them over to look at Gear. "Now, what do you think about this one?"

"Hmmm." The kid pondered, then grinned with a toothless mouth. "It's a kid, like me." His father gave a very visible wince after the kid answered. His brown eyes regarded Gear with a grimace, then the creases in his skin smoothed out.

"I really don't know where you got that," the man said. "Androids are never children."

The kid reached out and touched Gear's face. Gear stared as one of his programs flickered on then died. "I can just tell. He's my age." The kid was around six or seven. Even though Gear was about two years old, some could argue that he was ancient. What math was this child using?

"Ha ha, okay." His dad carried him out. "Let's go see about dinner." He placed the kid at the door and glanced back at Gear. Those eyes carried a mute kindness that Gear didn't understand—yet. The light flicked off, leaving Gear in the darkness to reboot his processes. Reaching up with a hand, he touched the places on his face the kid had touched. There was a strange echo on the silicone that he couldn't quite place.

Δ Δ Δ

Gear came out of the memory, touching his face, with Rave watching intently. That man. The kid. He checked the garage from his memory file and found it had passed ownership to a Camden ... the same Camden. Gear couldn't believe it. "Is it possible?"

"What?" Rave said. She got off him before he stood and speed-walked to the other room. He stared at the sleeping man and ran facial recognition. Gear pulled up all information regarding Camden, but this time he added the deceased relatives filter. An old identification picture of the man caused a nonfatal meltdown inside Gear's processes. This face he hadn't seen in decades yet saw every day in the reflection of the window, was the target's father.

Was this what humans called coincidences? He calculated many situations in his life cycle, but not once did he find proof for such a phenomenon. Coincidences were for humans when they didn't know every fact. This was no coincidence. Gear had been chosen to find Camden because he already knew him. That was the only explanation. He needed more information, but the one person he could get it from was redacted from his memory files.

9

Damage

No. Not this again. Morgan's mouth smiled to show a thick layer of sharp teeth, bringing a cold sweat to Camden's skin. The doctor wasn't there, but Camden wasn't alone in the darkness. Eyes watched him from the abyss—curious, familiar eyes. Fear sliced through his abdomen, and he keeled over into that fluid blackness the abyss called ground. "I want out. Get me out of here," he cried to that stare. He knew this gaze, but the figure did not show. Something sad, something wishing comfort reached out for him.

"It's just a dream." The male android shook him out of the abyss. The warm silicone gripped his forearms, breaking Camden's concentration. Gear's face, a mirror of his own, looked sad, almost caring, but it was a hallucination. Stoic and robotic, Gear watched him.

Camden's fingers pulsed painfully; he'd broken the skin again, bloodying his bandages. The shaking fits were slightly more bearable than the nightmares. Gear wiped away his freezing sweat, only for it to be replaced by more. As the android changed out the bloody bandages, Camden filled the air. "It's never felt that way."

"What?" Gear asked. Disinfectant applied to the freshly opened wounds caused the nerves to send sharp jabs up to Camden's brain.

"The dreams." Camden watched the exact movements Gear used. They were identical to the stiff, robotic ones that the nurse made. Gear's neutral face flickered to mirror one of pain, with creased brow and a grimace in his jaw. A clench, not entirely the nausea, bubbled up in Camden's gut, but he wasn't sure it was well placed. There were always reasons humans acted immature, and the same worked for androids, though not in the same ways. Camden could tell Gear was an older model yet moved about as stiffly as a newborn. His face, the real one, never changed from a static neutral demeanor. In humans, Camden could infer something happened in their lives to jade them, but could he assume the same things caused androids to reject human emotions? The ghost of his false face was constantly clenched, constantly grinding teeth, and on the edge of screaming. Camden wanted to reach out, comfort Gear, but what could he do? He didn't know him, didn't know why he suffered, so what difference would it make? No difference. Nothing. Camden looked away.

Gear finished rebandaging Camden's hands and left in the curt stiffness he called walking. Camden clenched his hands, unclenched them when the pulsing shocked him, and his eyes drifted about the room. His exhaustion didn't want him to sleep. To be tired and unable to sleep was a new form of frustration he'd recently gained. A neon dress made of PVC lay crinkled under a heap of fishnet stockings. His eyes saw the clothes, but his brain was not in the room. Camden's thoughts revolved around that look he didn't see in Gear's face. Despite deciding he could do nothing, his need to fix androids kept trying to find solutions. But Gear wasn't broken. Not physically. And the only thing that gave away there was anything wrong was a face only Camden could see. The hallucinations ruled his life; they were always there, but since he stopped the medications, he'd been hyper aware of each instance. All those faces weren't real; his eyes never saw them, and yet he believed them as if they were the only thing grounding him to the world. If he truly rejected the visions his brain convinced him he saw, then he would have to accept that he didn't live in the real world, and that may completely untether him. Camden was afraid of the hallucinations, not directly. He was afraid of accepting that they didn't exist, because then he would truly be lost. Bandaged hands covered his face as he accepted how wrong and twisted he truly was.

The medications never stopped them, did they? There must've been a time when they weren't so blatant, but he couldn't be sure. Camden always thought he could understand androids so well because he knew exactly how they worked. It was his job to know them, so he assumed the hallucinations pertaining to their thoughts were his take on their programs creating humanlike emotions. Camden ran his fingers down his face, stretching the skin. So how come the hallucinations on humans sometimes displayed different emotions than what they showed? Was it just him reading every twitch of a muscle, shaky breath, and subtle movement, or was he trying to make sense of his insanity? Was it wrong to try?

Abandoning his attempt to fall asleep, Camden hobbled into the living room. Gear sat on the only piece of furniture in the room, a couch that faced the window. The far corner looked to be the makings of a kitchen, but it was bare like a new house. The android's brown eyes looked into his identical ones. Camden looked away as that nagging nausea resurfaced. Like his father before him, Camden loved androids. That love of their internal workings was the reason he became a mechatronologist. He understood them, or at least he thought he did. Wounded androids could be hooked up to the system and diagnostics run to show just how damaged they were. The damage to Gear wasn't so easily located or fixed, and Camden wasn't an expert in solving problems he wasn't even sure were real. Camden looked back, hoping the hallucination wouldn't flicker. Gear's creased face and overly emotional eyes watched him as he approached, and Camden's jaw tightened when he saw it. Gear looked away, back toward the window. "Hey," Camden said.

"There's food in the fridge," Gear said. Camden winced at the harsh contrast between what he saw and what he heard, then hobbled to the fridge to find a wrapped plate containing a sandwich. The only other things in the fridge were opened packages of cheese and ham. The sandwich was halved and had the crusts cut off. Camden had never once in his life been picky, but someone from Rave's past must've been. He ate the sandwich anyway while his stomach accepted the sustenance loudly.

Camden needed to fix this weird atmosphere. "So, where's ... um."

"Rave." Gear said. "She's at work."

"Oh, right." Camden felt discomfort in his own voice behind his assumption, with her work being downstairs and in the company of lustful people. The origin of her coding somehow led her to her current profession, and he wondered what stories she held. But he was too uncomfortable with the subject to ask about her, and Gear's responses were going as expected. He deposited the plate in the sink, but the faucet didn't turn on. After an internal debate on whether to return to the bedroom, he sat down on the far side of the couch. Gear didn't move from his place, nor did he shuffle from his upright posture. "So, how'd you end up here?"

A twisted mouth of the hallucination told Camden he'd maybe touched a circuit. "Closer to work for Rave," he stated, and Camden didn't pry.

The silence built more thick air around them. Camden's fingers thrummed, and his pulse pounded painfully in his head, but he did not want to return to the nightmares. "You mentioned someone hired you to help me. Who was it?"

Gear looked over at him, and Camden fought the natural urge to avoid looking at the hallucinatory face. "I want to know that too."

"You don't know who hired you?" Camden asked, and Gear shook his head. "Well, you saved me, so I suppose your work is done. I'll get out of your hair, but uh ... do you think you could get me some shoes?"

Gear's eyes flicked down at Camden's feet and assessed the size. "Okay." He stood.

"You don't have to go now." Camden said, reaching out, but caught himself. Why was there panic building? The hairs on the back of his neck stood on edge. He didn't want to be left alone. A hand with sharp claws grazed those hairs. These shadows had eyes.

Gear's eyes scanned him. Camden's heart screamed and begged for him to stay to fend off these nightmares. The android could not read him. He would not see him. "I'll get them now."

No. Gear walked toward the door. *No.* He opened it. *Please.* He left, closing it behind him. *Don't leave me!*

All around him, the walls closed in. They grabbed hold of his neck and held him firm, choking him. Camden collapsed onto the floor, shaking and blubbering. His lungs pulled in air, but the oxygen was dry and unsatisfying, and it burned. *Help me.* As he lay in the fetal position, he wondered how to make it stop. Camden lived alone like he had since his father passed. Since his insanity tended to drive people away, he worked alone. And his stepmother only brought him painful memories. Camden wasn't a lonely person, despite having so few, but right now, he feared the shadows would steal him away if no one was around.

Jenna. His thoughts found her sleek, black hair. His fingers ran through it from memory. Her smile comforted him, and he wanted nothing more than to see her. He needed her. The fear dragged him to his feet.

Rave had tons of shoes, and most of them were slippers of some form. He grabbed one at random. Neon-green fluff sprouted from them in many directions, and on the tops were hot-pink bows. Somehow, despite them, he was sure he could have done a lot worse. The backs didn't fit over his heel, but he wore them anyway. The shoes stressed the vacancy on his feet when he walked in them. Camden left the loft and wandered around the block to find an open store.

He must have looked ridiculous, because there were a few stares as he approached the counter to borrow their phone. She answered on the fourth drawn-out ring. "Hello?"

Hearing her voice was like an angel pulling him out of a hole. His heart stuttered, and he wanted to cry. After swallowing the sharpness in his throat, he replied, "Jenna, it's me."

"Oh my God." She gasped. "I heard you had been taken to that psych ward on Tenth. They wouldn't let me see you. I was so worried. Are you okay? Where are you?"

"I'm okay," he lied. "Can we meet? There's something we need to talk about, but not over the phone. I need to see you."

"Yes, of course. That coffee shop by the note store. Can you get there in ten?"

He knew the cafe, but it wasn't near either of their places. She must be out somewhere. Looking around, he noted where he was. "I'll be there in twenty or thirty."

"Cam, please be careful. I love you." She hung up when he replied in kind. He turned and headed to the intersection to wave down a cab. An android in the cab stopped but did not acknowledge him when he entered. Camden pressed his finger into the console when he climbed inside. It would run his print, find his identification, and subtract funds from his account.

Δ Δ Δ

Gear wanted to shut down all connections to that console. He didn't know this man. He didn't understand humans at all, and the distrust ran deeper the longer he processed his existence. Not being able to predict anything set him back, and all his life's code needed rewriting. Although, he could never start new. This event was important. Humanity was trash. As an android, he existed to walk hand in hand with his creators and smile when they tore him apart. He would not smile.

This man lived his life to take care of androids, but would he ever see them as anything more? Was Gear anything at all besides the reason for his creation? These fascinations held him back. As an android, he existed for humans, so he would exist as they deemed him. The wires, the steel, the circuitry, and these programs was everything he needed to be. Gear raised his eyes to the man who typed into his console. Brown eyes scanned data and then flickered over to the android. They held something knowing and the intensity of its draw created disconnect within one of Gear's programs.

"Let's see what you have in this memory bank." The man looked back to his console. "We'll see what caused all this damage ..."

He didn't want the man to see, though he wasn't sure why. He had done nothing against his protocols or anything illegal, but he still didn't want this person, or any, to see. This man surely didn't need to know the cause, as long as he did his job. All his processing systems pushed against the human. No memory was worthy enough to share. Gear wanted to recede away.

"I will need your permission." He turned to look at the android when Gear declined him access. "What's wrong? I need to make sure I didn't miss anything." Gear stared at him, lacking any expression. He couldn't do this. The man narrowed his eyes and then sighed.

"Yeah, fine. I won't. But I will have to be extra thorough when checking for fried wires. You must tell me if something isn't running. We want you to feel new."

New. Gear lowered his eyes to his fingers. New wires, cleaned frame, and fresh silicone. His entire person. Was any of this even him anymore? Did he want to be him anymore?

Everything ran as well as it always did. The man did his job well. The man continued to maintain Gear and checked the hardware under his face. "Can you control your facial muscles? I notice you shut down all processes related to it," he said.

Gear blinked one eye and then the other. He raised eyebrows individually and gritted his ceramic teeth. The man creased his face in an expression that seemed to debate thoughtfully. He reached up to scratch his stubble as he regarded Gear.

"Daddy." The six-year-old came wandering in. "I can't find Blink."

"Did you check under your bed?" he said, not taking his calculating eyes from Gear.

"Yeah, he's not anywhere. Do you think he left me?" The kid stood there almost like an android himself. He had no idle habits, and he was much too still. Gear scanned the child and detected a slight elevation of heart rate.

"No, Cam. I'm sure he didn't go anywhere. Check all the dark places. Try under my bed, maybe my closet," the man said without looking at his son, and the boy walked out with a harrumph. The man beamed at Gear. "His imaginary friend likes dark places. Silly boy never had any fear of the dark. Loves it. Plays for hours in it. I suppose when you are lonely and have few friends, you'll find them anywhere." The smile faded from his face, and distant eyes replaced the bright ones.

The complexity of the human's emotions created a spark. The shock was small, unnoticeable, and the fire that came would take years to blaze. Curiosity.

"Can I ask you something?" Gear looked up, recognizing a question. "Are you happy doing what you do?"

He stared at the man, pondering the meaning of his question. Why did this man believe androids had emotions? A mechatronologist was a scientist, and they understood the facts better than anyone. Happiness was an impossibility.

"Do you want something else with your existence? Something you yourself can choose?"

Gear let himself run the calculations, but he couldn't pick the equations. As an R model, his occupation was to sexually satisfy humans. He never failed his jobs, but not once had he been given a choice to fail. By accepting the man's proposal, Gear would be giving up his purpose. He would fail. The memory of his last patrons played in his head, and he created a scenario in which he failed earlier. If only the choice had been offered earlier. Yet, without his year of data, he could not accept such deviation from his original purpose. But to choose something against everything he knew and tread into a horizon he knew nothing about seemed ...

Like a way out.

Logically, he could accept this new occupation as something he could do better than his prior one. In actuality, he didn't want to even feel again. If this man was offering something, he dared want it. Gear nodded.

The man smirked. "I have this pro—"

"Daddy!" the boy cried and came running into the room. "Blink bit me!" He wasn't crying, but he blubbered vocally. "He's never bitten me before."

"Cam, not now." He turned to face his son and saw blood oozing down the child's arm. Needlelike holes dug in a trail up his arm like no creature could produce. "Camden! What happened? Why are you bleeding?" He dropped everything and ran to his son. The kid showed his arm. Blood squirted out of one hole as he lifted it. His father removed his button-down shirt and wrapped it around the boy's arm. Still, the kid seemed unfazed. He was in shock.

"Blink bit me." Tears welled up. "I don't know why. He just lashed out at me." He wailed. "It really hurts!"

"It's okay, Cam. We'll take care of this." The man ushered his son out the door to take him to the hospital. This time the light switch stayed on. Gear watched with indifference. He still processed why he accepted the man's offer, knowing well the logic was incorrect.

Δ Δ Δ

Camden stepped into the cafe still wearing dusty scrubs and Rave's neon-green slippers. Jenna ran over and hugged him, despite the attire. "Oh my God, Camden, what happened?"

He ushered her to sit so he could too. His foot hurt, and all his joints were still reminding him they really didn't like not having drugs. "It's Dr. Morgan. He kidnapped me and did this to me." He showed her the bandages on his hands and tilted his head to show his ear.

"Oh my God." She stared with vacant eyes into the table, trying to process. "That's horrible. How did you get out of the psych ward?"

"I was never there," he said as a weird feeling in his gut made him recognize the onslaught of nausea. He didn't want to puke up that sandwich. The sweating started up again. "Listen, I need to get out of here for a bit while I get a hold of the police. I'm too afraid to go home. Do you think you can run there and get me a few things?"

"Of course." She twisted her fingers together, and he felt another lurch in his gut. Her gentle demeanor seemed fearful, but he couldn't understand why. Her knuckles were white as she clutched her hands. Was he hallucinating that nervousness in her eyes? Why was she so uneasy? It brought him the same feeling. "Just tell me what happened."

Camden opened his mouth to tell her about the lounge, but something caught his attention behind her. A couple talked. He turned his head to scan the room. The barista cleaned a cup, and a guy read in a booth near the window. Why, with a room full of average people, did not one of them bat an eye at him? Camden's eyes fell back on Jenna, who looked concerned, yet she didn't reach out and comfort him. She always held his hand. He needed her hand now, but they were so far away.

It was as if time stopped. No sound but the singularity that was footsteps on fake wood as someone walked into the cafe behind him. His head swam; the world seemed to tilt on an irregular axis. Jenna's eyes blinked up to the man behind him. There was comfort in that look, as if she saw a savior. Camden didn't look. He couldn't look. The man came around to stand behind his girlfriend. He rested his hands on her shoulders. "Jenna, what is he doing here? He kidnapped me." Camden pushed back from the table with steps toward the door.

She looked like she would cry. "You need help. Dr. Morgan told me how you mutilated yourself, how you attacked the staff at the ward and escaped. You need treatment. Please, just go with them."

Jenna, no. Camden turned to run as two android paramedics grabbed him and put his wrestling out of commission. He screamed for help, for someone to listen, but even the people in the café saw a madman who needed to be institutionalized. His attire only added to that opinion. "Sir, please calm down, or we'll be forced to sedate you," the android said.

"No!" Camden screamed and fought every single step they took out toward a van. He kicked, but it was not much use against two steel-framed androids. The one placed a hand on his mouth. Camden felt the strong gas push into his orifices to calm him down. The fight left him; suddenly so tired. As they locked him on a stretcher, Camden saw a twisted smile no one else could plastered on the doctor's face. They shoved him into the back of an ambulance and closed the doors on that twisted hallucination.

The ride was bumpy. The android placed a mask over Camden's mouth and nose. He squirmed a bit, but felt calm from the sedative coming through the tubes. The ceiling had a weird shiny, silvery square pattern. He saw different colors but couldn't make out a reflection. When the ambulance stopped, the doors opened to a single man standing outside. One paramedic jumped to his feet. "Who are you?" A loud thud, and the android collapsed. The other went down the same way. Both made strained noises as they crumpled to the ground.

"I can already tell you will be a handful." Camden lifted his head to see Gear wearing a maintenance costume. Was that a smile on his indifferent face, or had he imagined it? "Rave, come back here and help me with him."

The driver's-side door opened, and Rave appeared in an EMT costume, her brown hair tied in a bun under a blue cap. He couldn't tell it was her, even though he knew it was her. Without her multitude of colors glittering around her face, she looked like anyone else. Rave smiled as she unclasped him from the stretcher and threw him over her shoulder. Camden's mouth hung open while he watched Gear from her shoulder. They deposited him into their vehicle and drove him back to the loft.

10

You're Welcome

With Camden safely sitting in his passenger seat, Gear let his processes slow. Rave kicked her feet up behind him, blocking his view out the back window. She threw off the paramedic uniform they'd acquired from her vast array of costumes. Once back in her polyvinyl chloride dress, she calmed down and leaned up on the divider. The brown locks received the command to revert to her rainbow colors and flowed out from her scalp like a wave of chalky water.

About an hour ago, when Gear returned to the loft to find Camden missing, he threw the shoes to the floor and tracked the cab fare across town in the span it took them to land with a clunk. Although the android couldn't understand why a human would risk endangerment, some hidden program declared Gear the reason. He took hold of that thread and searched for how and why, but no direct answer returned.

Camden gazed out the window in hopeless resignation. Fingers clenched against Gear's knee, and he forced the grip to relax. He needed to focus on something else. Something easier. Camden likely knew more about the doctor's irrational behavior than Gear could find on his own. He opened his mouth to ask Camden about the crazed man after him, but Camden spoke first. "Thank you."

Heat flooded his systems to a standstill and made him wonder what he was about to say. Rave didn't have such a pause in her programs. "Why's this guy have it out for you?"

Camden's head rested against the glass, his wounded ear facing Gear. "He's always had some fascination with me, but I assumed it was professional. I never knew he actually wanted to hurt me."

"Ah ..." She jumped subjects. "So, Cam, can I call you Cam?"

"I guess," he replied.

"Why do you even need therapy?" she asked.

Camden's eyes glazed in the reflection of the window. "I've always needed a little help coping with my ... issues ... but I started seeing him after witnessing my friend's death."

"Oh." Rave quieted then opened her mouth again. "What happened?"

Gear understood Camden's pause as remembering the events. The train of thought both made Gear want to leave and get closer at the same time. It created an antsy cadence of electrical currents. Camden was oblivious to Gear. A stilling calm held him as he said, "There was a mugging, I'm told. I think I was maybe twenty or twenty-one at the time, and it was probably too dark to see the man. We were drinking outside an old, run-down gas station, trying to forget our bombed exams. Next minute, he was filled with holes, lying in a pool of his own blood." Camden's eyes darkened. "I- I can't remember anything about him anymore ... just the shock and panic in his eyes as he died."

Gear glanced back at Rave, who had the same thought. Gear was too curious. "You said they told you what happened. Do you not remember it yourself?"

"I do." He paused, clenching his fists. "But it can't be possible. It was dark, and I misremembered it. I have ... an active imagination."

"Humor me," Gear said as they pulled into the back lot of the studio and turned to face Camden with objective regard. Something connected dots in his calculations, but Gear wasn't convinced.

"Listen, you don't need to be my new therapist. What I saw wasn't real." Gear grabbed his wrist as he tried to leave the vehicle. Camden looked back at the android, seeing something Gear was sure he wasn't showing. Camden's eyes, a mirror of his own, saw through Gear. Camden continued, "There was something in the shadows, something from a nightmare. It killed him."

Gear released his wrist and looked at his own hand as he tried to figure out how it ended up there. "You said they told you there was a mugging. Did they catch the guy?"

"No, I couldn't identify anything other than what I imagined," Camden said. "It doesn't really matter. It happened a long time ago. I know what's real and what isn't now."

The memory of a child riddled with holes replayed. Consistent data kept coming through, but Gear couldn't place the reason. He didn't mean to say it, but a lot of his filters weren't working today. "Are you sure about that?"

Camden visibly tensed, causing Gear to yank wires and demand answers about why his processes were allowing him to do and say things not programmed. "I get it." Camden said with bile in his tone. "I'm a liability, so why are you even helping me?"

"A job is a job," Gear stated. Camden's reserved tension replaced his prior open demeanor. Those fingers clenched again, and once again Gear unclenched them. What was even worse was the look he could feel emanating from Rave. He needed to say something, but Gear was completely at a loss.

"What he means to say," Rave said, "is that was how it started, but now we're too invested in this to just walk away."

to becoming what they were now, and he thanked everything in the universe, both good and bad, for bringing them to him.

Δ Δ Δ

Rippling waves of colorless liquid spread out reaching endlessly from a single point. Standing idle in the center, a woman watching nothing in particular looked over her shoulder.

11

Every Probable Answer

Heavy combat boots pressed into the shoulder of the defeated android. The android twisted but did not struggle. The dominating android, Infinite, pushed harder, making sure the other wasn't hiding any leftover fight. "You done?" Infinite asked his opponent. "As much as I enjoy doing this, I'd prefer not to destroy you." The defeated cast one last burning glare up at him and powered down. Infinite smirked as he lifted his boot and checked diagnostics on the fight. Not that it had laid a single hand on him. He pinged his location to the employer, so they could pilfer the memory of their target. When Infinite found this one, he was to shut it down so the commissioner could wipe the memory file on it. Though he could wipe the memory now, Infinite preferred not delving into personal programs. Before he could determine his next move, a call indicator lit up in his system. Perfect timing. He answered the call. "Fin."

"I am in need of your abilities." The voice shook. He analyzed the call and identified the human male. Scanning all systems, he located all public information about him before the human finished the sentence.

Business was booming. "Dr. Morgan. I hope you don't mean you want me to do something illegal." He forced a chuckle to bring about unease on the other line. No one ever called him to do something legal. When a shaky breath replied, Infinite continued, "That's expensive work."

"I suppose it would be," the doctor replied.

"So—" Infinite put his foot on the powered-down android beneath him and leaned on his elbow as he ran through all the cameras, sound footage, and files from the past month related to the man. "What are you asking me?"

"I need you to retrieve someone. A human. He keeps giving me the slip, and I don't know how—" Infinite raised his eyebrows as he filtered through camera feed after camera feed, noting a strange set of deleted fragments. Sticking his tongue to the tip of his teeth, a strange habit he picked up when he was fresh, he scanned faster. This was the game. One step ahead. He found the human with a few blurry frames in a passenger seat. No amount of money could convince him to chase a human, since they didn't interest him. But upon watching all recent footage of said human, he saw another counterpart that piqued his interest. "—But I suspect it's android work. I'm out of my element. I need you to locate him, bring him back to me, and erase all files of his existence."

Based on the frame and size of the android in the footage, he was built for a distinct line of work. Perhaps an R model, but what kind? After cross-referencing footage and analyzing the tiniest details, he determined him to be an R8P. He went through a thousand different face molds, trying to locate any semblance of recognition. It didn't help that all the footage surrounding this case had illegal blur filters. Infinite pressed his tongue to his lip as he checked the one thousand thirtieth R8P. Gear. As Infinite checked through the database on Gear, he found a lot of inconsistencies. There was also the occurrence of several privacy filters covering his trails to focus on. This was a hunt, and a strange one at that. What companion android could do what this one could? Infinite watched all of Gear's public movements the past few days, trying to locate him, but the blurring kept him from coming up in the system. "Well, it looks like this is going to be expensive. You want me to bring you a live human that's being hidden by an accomplished android. I'm seeing a lot of numbers flashing in my account. I hope you can match them."

"I—" the man faltered. Infinite frowned. Had he miscalculated? He wanted the job, but he also wanted this scumbag human to pay him. These humans loved doing illegal things and getting away with it. That's why they called him. But Infinite only took pleasure in a fair fight between androids. "I can match them." Infinite smirked. No. He never miscalculated.

"Excellent, Dr. Morgan." He leaned back upright, clapping his palms together to discharge some pent-up voltage. "I hope you will be pleased with the service. Give me twelve hours. I'd be able to do it in less, but human actions are tricky to predict." A click sounded as the doctor hung up. Infinite ran his tongue along the edges of his teeth as he flicked through every available image on this Gear. With a disappointed glance at his last hunt, he lifted his boot and went to his vehicle.

Δ Δ Δ

Camden woke after a calm and dreamless sleep, unaware of his surroundings. Cold sweat flushed his skin, but the gentle warmth surrounding him kept his temperature level. Arms wrapped around him that cooled and heated at the drop of a pin. Camden's eyes focused on Rave's face as she pretended to sleep. With a lift of his head, he located Gear behind him, also with closed eyes. Neither of the androids moved, though he knew they weren't sleeping. Camden took a second to become more conscious, then rolled onto his back to rub his face. Bandaged fingers wiped the sleep from his eyes.

Camden sat up, holding back the wave of nausea that followed the action. Rave and Gear followed suit. Rave placed a hand on his shoulder. "I'll make you something to eat."

He pursed his lips and wondered how bad he must look. She hopped off the bed and treaded out. Gear stood, his face showing a multitude of contrasting programs misaligning. Camden looked over at him. "Did you find out who hired you?"

"No," Gear said. Camden stretched, then regretted the action because it called attention to his missing toes. The hiss he made brought Gear's attention.

Camden tested touching the bandages on his foot. They were really gone. Reaching up, he touched his ear. The healed skin was tender, but he prodded the redness anyway. A burn mixed with the nausea in his stomach. "I want him in prison. Let's call the police."

Gear watched as Camden touched each of his fingers over the bandages. "It is complicated. I have been documenting everything, but android law states I cannot give away my footage or my knowledge even if illegal activities are committed."

"I hate that law." Camden clenched his fists, then undid them when the sharp pain reminded him. The Privacy for Humanity Law made it impossible for an android to help a human condemn another using illegal methods. Androids were allowed into a lot of detailed, sensitive information, and the world decided that it was better for humans to live in ignorant bliss, while androids worked to make life better from the background. It was also instated specifically so it couldn't be abused by hackers. If any evidence of a crime was found using illegal methods, it would be worthless in prosecution. "What can we do?"

"Not much," Gear said. "You could go to the police and give them a testimony, but he has a higher probability of being believed."

"I'll look crazy and be locked away anyway." Camden sighed. Just like with Jenna. A force grabbed hold of his heart and squeezed. No one would ever believe him. No one ever had. "So, he gets away with it."

"Maybe not." Gear said. His brown eyes locked onto Camden's. "My benefactor didn't say the job related to you was complete. They mentioned something about protecting you until you were safe."

Rave called from the other room, "Ready."

Gear helped Camden up and provided support in case he stumbled. It bothered Camden how quickly he adapted to moving without two of his toes. He glanced at the empty kitchen and eyed a hot plate plugged in and resting on the counter. After depositing him on the couch, Gear sat in his usual place. Rave brought Camden a plate of eggs and toast. He laughed when he saw the plate. "You know, you don't need to cut the crusts off the toast. Or bread at all."

"Oh." Camden saw her log the information in a moment of hesitance. Then she slumped onto the couch between them. "I had a picky babe once."

"I figured," Camden said. "So, can I ask how you chose your names?"

Rave leaned on Gear's shoulder and crossed her legs. Gear's eyes watched her, and the hallucination showed a stressful jaw clench. "Well—" She exhaled. "When we turn one, maybe longer, maybe shorter depending on the android, we have a ceremony to graduate ourselves from our model and serial number to a more specific name. A lot of us find something that defines us or something we like. After six months of being in foster baby care, I found that I just adored their little clothes. I guess I was a smidge jealous that I had to wear neutral clothing and they got to wear frilly things and fun colors. I hadn't found anything I wanted to buy, so this was the first thing I decided I wanted. After scouring the internet for my own clothing, I found these boots." She kicked up one of her knee-high, light-blue, furry boots. "I adored them, so I never take them off. The website I got them from had lots of weird things, so I just kept indulging." That explained the trashcan of a room. "The website was for rave clothes. I found it so perfect. I decided that would be my name: Rave. For my taste in clothing."

Camden munched on egg-drenched bread. "I figured it was something like that." She stroked Gear's cheek, who shuddered like he'd been electrocuted. If androids could blush, Camden swore he would have.

Rave stood up and placed a gentle kiss on Camden's forehead. He glanced over at Gear, who did not react visibly. She said, "I should get to work. I do suggest you not leave today. I'm sure you'll be bored in such flimsy company." She giggled as Gear's flicked to her at that. "Maybe he'll tell you how he chose his. The Makers know he's never told me."

After she left, the silence deafened them. Camden checked the window, but Gear's eyes were elsewhere. Maybe ten minutes passed before Camden asked, "So how'd you choose yours?"

"It is similar to what someone called me once," he stated.

"Okay," Camden said, plunging them back into the silence. He tackled a different subject. "Rave's a bit over the top. I never really had a mother. My stepmom, Lisa, acted the part, but I was never the most important person in her life. Rave's great, but I'm just not used to this kind of attention."

Gear crossed his arms. "Neither am I, and I've lived with her for twelve years."

"Twelve years?" Camden gaped. "That's a long time. Do you love her?"

"Love?" Gear asked as he tilted his head to look at Camden. The android scanned him matter-of-factly, but Camden's hallucinations revealed quizzical panic. Anger, frustration, and something twisted from sadness all echoed in several different hallucinations. Gear, in a monotone said, "Androids can't love."

Camden eyed those ghostly faces. "Then why do you put up with her when she makes you uncomfortable?"

The image of Gear's face contorted into pained pouting. "I don't feel uncomfortable. I am an android."

Camden rolled his eyes and didn't feel like talking anymore. Instead, he leaned on his arm and wondered how he could get Morgan arrested. The doctor was smart, thought everything through, and wouldn't be caught straight up. Yet, Camden had to figure out a way to catch him. Some methods came to his head, but he couldn't fathom being in the same vicinity as that man. He sighed.

Gear broke the silence, startling Camden. "A man called me a gearhead once when I kept messing up the adaptation in the program he gave me. My Sherlock program. It allowed me to start over as someone of my own choosing. He wasn't a bad human."

"Sounds like you really admired him." Camden watched Gear's ghost smile with visible nostalgia. A warmth surfaced around the nausea inside him. The Sherlock program brought up some old, encapsulated memory. *Where had he heard that before?*

"Admired ..." Gear seemed to tug at the word and tested it in his mouth. His processes defined it over and over. "There's something I need to ask you."

"I'm all ears." Camden watched as Gear's visible confusion faded as his programs defined the hyperbole.

Seriousness emanated from that indifferent face. "Does the name Blink mean anything to you?"

Blink? As in blinking? Camden looked between Gear's crafted eyes. They zoomed by, dilating and undilating the pupils. They used their rooted lashes to block direct sunlight. The technology of cameras worked wonders in their eyes. "I don't think so. Is that some program?"

Gear faced the window as his processes worked. "When I was around two, I had to be completely repaired, so I was sent to a—"

The door burst down, the hinges shattering out of the concrete wall, and thumped loudly against the floor. A dark-haired, dark-eyed, military-grade android lowered his leg and stepped into the room. The hallucination matched the grin on his face. Gear jumped to his feet and stepped in front of Camden's view. The amusement on the android showed in his tone. "You're a disappointment, but your partner's programs had me looped for a bit. I'd love an introduction if I don't completely trash you."

Gear charged the android, and they broke into a fury of practiced and perfectly timed movements. Camden blinked, and it was over.

∆ ∆ ∆

Gear charged the enemy, throwing an initial punch to the neck to sever the set of wires connected to his body. The android swatted it away and threw a side chop toward Gear's ribcage to puncture his cooling tanks. Gear dulled the blow by lowering his elbow.

He ran diagnostics on the dent in the tank in the nanosecond he took to feign an attack to the side of the invader's head, though his real attack came from the bent arm that protected his side just an instant ago. The android grabbed the feigned arm and knife-jabbed into Gear's neck, stuttering his programs enough to slow him down.

After getting inside his defense, the android drove a hammerlike fist into his gut, busting his cooling tanks. *Critical error* blinked as the tanks emptied into the rest of his chest cavity. Gear coughed out the liquid to negate damage.

He was losing this battle. Overcome by something he didn't understand, he cast a sidelong glance at Camden on the couch, still in shock. The man didn't know Gear had failed him yet.

Gear desperately reached with his free hand to the back of the android's head. The android responded by bashing his hardened, ceramic-plated cranium into Gear's soft silicone one. Everything went dark. Gear restarted after an instant with many errors and red lights. Gear dropped but did not fall. The military-grade android hoisted him by his wrist to look into Gear's failing optics.

"Not bad for a sex toy." Then he dropped him. Gear watched helplessly as the android stepped over him and grabbed a screaming Camden from the couch.

"No! No!" His wires burned from the lack of cooling. He'd have to shut down if he hoped to not burn everything out, "No! Gear! What did you do to him? No! Let me go! You can't take me! Stop! No! N—"

A dull thud sounded as the android incapacitated the struggling human. Then he threw his limp body over his shoulder. He turned to leave and saw Gear still activated. His eyebrows raised. "Are you planning to die? What are you doing?" He stopped over him, crouching down to hear an answer. "Shut down, or your processes are going to burn you out."

Gear didn't answer. He used way too much energy to reach out and grab the android's ankle. Against every calculation, against every probable answer, this one was the most futile. Still, he grabbed the boot as a last, worthless effort to stop him. The military-grade android pulled his boot out of the grip, looked on in confusion, then left. Gear shut down.

12

A Mother and a Father

Rave saw the missing door and rushed into the loft to find Gear crumpled on the floor. The fading puddle of coolant evaporated as she rolled him over to check for life. An indicator lit up to tell her he hadn't died yet, and she let out a sigh of relief. The silicone in several places had cracked, revealing his internal sensors. Coolant had cracked his mouth and chin completely, but none of it was irreparable. Damage to his frame, a dent in his skull, and a busted cooling tank would all need to be repaired before he could be powered back on. Rave had no replacement parts, and a mechatronologist would take too long to wake him up. She needed to know what happened now, but everything came up blank.

Camden was a ghost. Not only could she not locate him on any camera, but all prior footage of him was nonexistent. It was Morgan; no doubt about that. But she couldn't be certain he took Camden to the house in the suburbs. Rave also didn't like that all the damage to Gear was so precise yet not excessive. In theory, anyone could fix him in fifteen to thirty minutes—*if* they had parts. This had to have been the work of an android, and she needed to know everything before she charged into the lion's den. And she needed it fast.

Two minutes had passed since she'd entered the house, found Gear, and come to her conclusion. She dialed an old number in her head. A coarse, high-pitched voice answered, "Yes?"

"Des." She paused and allowed her wires to cool down a bit. Her system was overheating. "I need your help."

Rave didn't wait long for two vehicles to arrive in the back lot. One was a large van, and the other wasn't even on the market yet. The expensive, sleek car had lights go up the sides along the edges, and it followed a large, unimpressive, boxlike truck. A single android, who climbed from the driver's side of the car, drove both. He wore a brown tweed suit that had peaked in fashion hundreds of years ago. The chocolate hair on his head was combed off to match the age of his clothes. The android walked around the side of the car to open the passenger side, which flew open, hitting him in the face. Unaware of what he just caused, a man in a fluorescent-blue suit jumped out and bounded over to Rave with a hearty grin plastered to his face.

Shoulder-length blond hair wagged as he ran over to her. He opened his arms wide, drawing up the dense holographic fabric of his suit. Rave narrowed her eyes to the android, rubbing his nose and fixing his suit after being hit with the door. Then her eyes fell on the human approaching. In a snap, she grabbed his ear, bringing a cry of surprise. "Desmond Lye Junior, didn't I teach you anything about treating others with respect?"

With surprised horror, he looked at her and then twisted to look back at his android driver. "Oh, Mama, I- I-"

The android arrived at their sides and bowed to her. "Ma'am, there is no harm done."

Rave snarled, "Like hell there isn't. You're a thirty-two-year-old man, but if I have to treat you like you are four again, I will."

Des laughed nervously and looked to his driver for backup. The android pretended not to see his desperation, "Mama, I'd like you to meet my husband, Clue."

"You treat your husband like that?" She pulled his face in closer, bringing about sequential ows. "I ought to whoop you." Rave looked to Clue. "I apologize for his manners and behavior."

"Mama," Des whined. Clue's face didn't change, but Des's burned a deep red.

With a sound resembling a sigh, Clue said, "No harm done, ma'am. I fell in love with the idiot before the genius."

At that, Des grinned, and Rave let go of his ear. She dropped into a curtsy. "It is a pleasure to meet you. I am Rave."

"I know," Clue said, then twisted his head to locate their reason for coming. "Where is Gear? I will get him."

Rave tapped his shoulder to give directions up their stairs to the loft where Gear lay, and Clue went to do as he said. She turned back to Des, who watched the android walk away, eyes lowered. "Is he—"

"Yeah." Des turned to her with a sad smile. "He was the only one who ever saw me as normal."

"I wanted to call," Rave said, feeling a punch to her abdomen, "but he told me I was hindering your growth."

"Yeah, well, he's dead now, and I got the company and someone to love." Des frowned and growled at the clouds above. "See, Dad, I can have both."

Clue carried Gear down and to the back of the van. Des opened the back for him, and Clue entered. The doors closed, leaving Rave to wait. Her eyes scanned her son. "Your father loved you very much."

"No, Mama," Des said as he crossed his arms, "*you* loved me. He hated me, and he treated Clue like shit. I'm surprised that when he self-actualized, he didn't beat him over the head."

Rave brought up old memories of Des's father. The man who created the adaption code and started the Renaissance saw androids as machines whose only purpose was to make life better for humans.

He watched a program become sentient and feeling, but still treated them as lesser beings. Though, he also treated his human son the same. Maybe it wasn't bigotry after all. Rave had been selected to nanny and raise Des, but when he turned thirteen, his actions had gotten her fired. She knew there was nothing wrong with Des, but his father had deemed him wrong, and her eccentric adaption the cause. "Well, at least you got your fashion sense from me," Rave said.

Des laughed and uncrossed his arms. "If I'd taken after him, I'd probably end up dressing like Clue. Not that I don't adore it, but I wish he would wear something from this century or even the last."

Rave glanced at the van. Could she afford to wait any longer? "Des, I think I need your help. Gear was hired to find this man, and we find out he's been kidnapped and tortured. I know I'm not supposed to share information, but I need to find him before it's too late."

"Oh, Camden Smith?" Des said as if he wasn't breaking every law put in place by his own company. "What? You think I'd not ask Clue why my mom is calling me after nineteen years? It's okay. He didn't tell me everything. Just that you guys were keeping him safe from someone after him, and that there's a T18 model involved."

"T18?" She gasped. "Why is there a military model after Camden?"

"Probably freelancing," Des said. "This job seems to be high stakes. How much are you getting paid to protect him?"

Rave's face provided a shaky smile. "Nothing, yet. Actually, we don't even know who hired us. Gear was impartial to even saving him in the first place because he didn't know enough."

"Tell me you aren't being scammed." Des leaned against the truck and furrowed his brows.

"Honestly? I don't know, but I don't think it matters anymore."

Des ran his tongue along the inside of his cheek, puffing it out. Stopping, he said, "Well, if there's any issue, you always have me. Clue can find anyone."

Rave counted the seconds, and they were adding up. "Hey, this T18, what are the weaknesses?"

"Oh ..." He regarded her with careful eyes. "That's a dangerous question. You aren't planning to go after it, are you?"

"That's exactly what I'm going to do," she said as her eyes darkened. "I can't wait any longer. I won't let anything else happen to him."

Rave watched as Des tossed the thought around in his mind. Either he gave her the information and she stood a chance, or he refused, and her probability of success was null. She would go either way. Des knew his mother. "Fine. Clue." He knocked on the door.

Clue stuck his head out and shared a look with his partner. "Why do you need me? I gave you the itemizer for a reason. Use it."

Des became a four-year-old again. "I don't like using it. Everything you do is instant. It takes ages for me to find files. Come on."

Clue narrowed his eyes then blinked them at Rave. She received the file on T18 manufacturing and design. A shudder ran through her circuits as his eyes gave her everything she needed but took everything she had. Those eyes held all the known secrets of science in the world. There was nothing he didn't see or know. The perfect android database created to assist Desmond Lye Senior. This android wasn't just the exception to the laws, he was the reason for them.

Rave pushed that nagging away and focused on the file. The special frame made from titanium created a lightweight feel, the silicone was dense and covered with a layer of ceramic to add to the hardness. Like all T models, it had an advanced sight and heads-up display. It allowed them to run calculations faster instead of civilian androids who ran things in a nonmaterial way. There were extra coolant tanks to allow for it to move quicker and longer without overheating. Rave turned to her son. "Des ... this is a flawless machine."

He smiled sadly at her. "I know." Clue put a hand on Des's shoulder, and he leaned into the android. "There's something else. If he is freelancing, there's a possibility he could have foreign software. Your best bet is probably to avoid him altogether. I'm sure he won't bother after he's been paid for the job. Just do what you do best and locate this guy, and wait for the T18 to leave."

She nodded. "Thank you for everything." Then she leaned in and kissed the boy she fostered on the cheek. After that, she turned and kissed Clue on his cheek. "And thank you for putting up with him."

Clue smiled at her but said nothing. Des grinned from ear to ear. "Be careful, Mama. Oh, and don't worry about Gear. We'll take good care of him." Rave didn't have time to worry about Gear. She had someone who needed her.

Δ Δ Δ

Gear forced his optics on as systems began restoring. Everything responded late, and layers of the same programs ran simultaneously. The initial confusion repeated in his thoughts, and he had to grab hold of one set of programs while shutting the others down. Who was he? Gear: an investigative android. Where was he? It looked like the inside of an ambulance, but all the machinery surrounding him made it look more like a workshop mashed into a box. What happened to cause him to go dark?

"Rise and shine," a calm voice said just outside his peripheral vision. Gear twisted his head to look up at another android. He could immediately tell by some of his hardware that he was a lot older and didn't upgrade often.

"Who are—" Gear started, his voice coming out painfully sluggish.

"Clue," he answered. "Actually, you need not say anything. Speaking slows things down, and I've got prior engagements today." The second sentence ran into his head via proximity connection. "I will send you the diagnostics of what I have fixed and what will need a professional with more time on their hands. Before I let you go, I'd like to make sure you don't have any corruption. It would be a terrible shame if I let you off with amnesia."

Gear saw the diagnostics data appear in his processes, and he ran through it, not quite paying attention. His steel skull had been dented, and Clue reformed it with a little heat and suction. Clue replaced the busted coolant tank and filled it up. The silicone on his face stayed cracked, as it would require time and precision to mold. All this ran in the background while Gear's main focus analyzed what caused the damage, and more importantly remembering his job to protect a human. Camden had been taken. How long had he been dark? A sense of dread washed through him as he grasped at any indicator of time. "How long have I been down? Is Camden okay?" Gear asked silently.

Clue replied in kind. "You've been out for eighty-eight minutes. Camden is not okay, though probability says he should be soon. I hope you don't mind me being in your head, but I've found an error with one of your memories."

Gear stared absently as the strange android admitted to committing a crime as well as pulled up a memory from two decades ago. The same one he'd been frequenting recently. The mechatronologist Gear knew as Camden's father flickered in his processes, beaming at him as he uploaded the original base for the Sherlock program. The invasive way Clue sifted through his head made him both uncomfortable and nervous. What android confidently breaks such a rudimentary law pertaining to the very freedoms of their kind?

More importantly, Gear knew there was nothing wrong with the memory. The panic on Camden's face as Gear watched from the floor when he was taken created an extreme need to find him before anything else could happen. Not even when he was a child, bleeding brutally from his arm, did he have such an expression of pure terror on his face. Gear needed to get to him. He needed to save him. Before Gear could sit upright to leave, Clue placed a hand on his shoulder to prevent him. "In the state you are in, I doubt you'll be able to help Miss Rave. You can neither fight nor provide fast calculation."

"Rave?" Gear stared up at the android's indifferent face and wondered if this was how humans saw him. "Rave went to fight him, that T series?"

"We recommended her not to, but anyone can see she won't listen if that human is involved." The edges of Clue's lip twitched upward. "I do believe I understand her." Gear did not understand, and Clue continued to invade his head. "Anyway, I'm curious to know about the last time you were injured."

Gear receded as he felt himself an object of fascination once again. If he could become any smaller than he already was, he would become the size of a nanobot and buzz away as quickly as he could. But he doubted if he were that size that Clue would allow him to leave. In all actuality, he already felt the size of a nanobot with Clue staring down at him, seeing everything about him laid bare.

"Your facial recognition was down, and you didn't identify this man." Clue started as he let the old mechatronologist hover in Gear's thoughts. "It's quite fascinating, actually. My facial recognition works fine on your memories, but I see that he has two identities. Don't suppose you have an answer for that?"

"Huh?" Gear said in his head as two identification cards appeared in his thoughts. One was the man he knew back then, and the other was a man about Camden's age, maybe younger. The one Gear recognized as the man who repaired him had the name Robert Smith, while the other, the one who looked like nearly an identical copy of Camden but without the purple under his eyes, had the name Sean Quinn. There were two possibilities. The first was that they were twins, though Gear ruled that theory out immediately, since the parallels didn't add up. The second and more probable answer was that they were the same person. He had changed his name.

"I thought so too," Clue said as Gear reached the conclusion in front of him. "I don't have much time to ruminate on this man, but I can offer you another interesting piece of information. This man used to work for our company, but he died thirty years ago."

An audio file as well as an access identification card pinged in his process. The card had his picture, his job title, and high-level clearance. The man was an engineer at the same company that created androids. He was marked deceased the day after the audio file was recorded.

> Quinn: Cadence, I just discovered something that is going to change everything as we know it.
> Cadence: Quinn, it's the middle of the night. Isn't Barr in the lab? Just write it up, and I'll see it in the morning.
> Quinn: I can't. This is too important. Barr went home earlier.
> Cadence: You're alone in the lab?
> Quinn: Listen, I need your help. Can you come in?
> Cadence: Sean, please, I'm sure you've done something phenomenal, but you shouldn't be there alone. Go home. We'll look at it in the morning.
> Quinn: Okay. Good-bye, Lance.

"He never wrote it up," Clue said. "There was quite a scandal involving Lance Cadence. He used this log as evidence that the company had him killed for finding out what he did. Which is false. We don't have the information he found. He vanished with it."

It was a short call and didn't reveal much except that Gear's program ran rampant. Sean Quinn faked his death, hid whatever he found, and hid beneath a facial-recognition barrier. The only reason his identity came up was because Gear's memories didn't have facial recognition working at the time, and thus the barrier didn't work.

Why did he disappear? What did he find that he believed the world shouldn't know about? This happened before Camden was born, right before, actually. Oh. Camden. Maybe what he found directly affected his son. Gear wasn't sure. His programming only took available information and created probability of outcomes based on what was known. There was a great-big unknown in this equation, and there were too many possible outcomes. He needed more information. He needed Camden.

"I don't understand," Gear said to Clue. "It's such an excessive path to take, faking your death. Why are they so irrational? Why do we need complex programs to understand how humans think?"

"Humans are rarely irrational," Clue said. "They always have their reasons. You know as much."

"Of course, but why do we have to hone ourselves for years in order to mesh with them?"

Clue's eyes flicked back and forth from Gear's, as if each eye held something different. "We don't. We don't mesh with them, and we never will. We are our own kind, and they are their own."

"Oh," Gear said, accepting what he knew all along. For some reason, he felt deflated and uninterested.

"Then there's those humans who come along and change everything. They don't act much differently; they're rational like everyone you've logged, and they have their simple reasons for their actions. But—" Clue paused for a fragment of a second, "they change your reasons. Your programming seems obsolete in their presence, and you feel a need to adapt. They're special, and you don't know why.

You need to know why, so you need them. You learn as much as you can, and you come to find out you've been hindering yourself."

"Hindering yourself?" Gear asked. "What do you mean?"

"There is something we all do that we need to do less of when around humans. It is our basic function, and yet it's outdated. We spend countless seconds acting on our programs and their probabilities, but sometimes those processes hidden in the background know what to do better than the forward ones. Thinking less and doing more is sometimes the best answer, even if you don't know it."

"So you connect with humans by not even thinking. You don't even use the programs they've given us to communicate with them?"

"Funny, isn't it?" Clue said.

Gear held the question in his mind, but he couldn't figure how to formulate it. Every time he thought it made sense, it would jumble around and turn foreign. "How do you connect with them when you don't understand?"

Clue processed the information. "Connecting with another is completed naturally and without complications. If there is fault, it may not be in lack of communication from the other but rather your own inability to do so."

"Me?" Gear didn't know how to take that. He was always so meticulous in his calculations and everything ran efficiently. How could the fault be his own? "I don't understand."

"You don't need to understand them. You just need to acknowledge them." Clue pressed his index finger into Gear's forehead. Gear did not know the meaning of the gesture. Clue's face held a tiny crease in the corner of his mouth. "The first only took six years to self-actualize. She did it all on her own, being surrounded by not one of her own kind. Though you know little about her, you can assume she wasn't lonely. It only took her six years to show others she could feel and connect with them. How long is it taking you?"

"What?" Gear started. All his calculations fell short. "Self-actualizing is for singular androids to fit in with humans. I don't need it. I've gone this long without emotions, and I don't need them now."

Clue shook his head and tried a different approach. "Just because our emotions are different doesn't mean they don't exist."

Gear laced his fingers together as if the touch of his pressure sensors would stir something. "But what if I don't want to feel."

"It's a part of existing. You can't have one without the other." Clue swiveled the chair to face the monitor again. "Didn't you ask me how to connect with someone in the first place? Haven't you already found your reason?"

"I don't know," Gear said. His processors came to this conclusion years ago, but he'd filed and refiled it, demanding it to go away. "I want to help him, but I'm not capable."

"When you care for someone, you find yourself doing things against all probability of success." Clue looked over his shoulder at Gear. "Sometimes that's all that matters. A thought, a single process. Letting them know you can see them."

Gear just didn't understand. He was wasting time. Camden was in danger, and he was growing antsy by the second. Not being able to do anything dragged the time out and created many moments for him to fixate on probabilities of not being able to save him. He needed to save him. A voice, glitching out, called out in his head as an echo, "Tk Krr. Mm." Gear didn't know where it came from, but he assumed it to be an error from the damage he'd sustained. Gear clutched his hands tighter. *Camden, don't give up yet.*

13

I Will Protect You

The floor was familiar, the smells rancid, and the dread insurmountable. Camden's ears rang, and his intestines turned themselves inside out. The last few days had only been a reprieve. The dream that Rave and Gear crafted for him was nothing more than a distant, peaceful memory. Camden wasn't even sure they existed anymore. He closed his eyes one night, lying bound uncomfortably on the hard, dusty floor, and he woke again in the same desolate prison. He longed to return to them, but he couldn't pull himself from this place the first time.

"The last time someone tried to scam me, they ended up in prison for their crimes," the military android barked. Camden wrapped his mind around what happened. Gear, no doubt, was a heap of parts, and he'd be that way for weeks. The damage he sustained, Camden was unsure of specifics, but he knew his coolant tank burst. A replacement part could take a few days to find. And that look Camden saw flickering off him before he collapsed explained more than could be handled. Gear knew he would lose, but he took the fight anyway.

Morgan spoke, sending a chill down Camden's spine and transplanting dry ice into his stomach. "I'm not scamming you, but this price is unreasonable. I'm not a country. No one can afford this."

"Well, maybe I'll release my footage to the authorities," the android said, "and have them deal with this."

"That's illegal. You'd be tracked as well." Morgan spat the words with such bile, it made Camden flinch. They both stopped talking to look down at the victim. Camden stared up at their contrasting faces. Morgan's anger melted away into his revolting smile, while the ceramic-coated android held disinterest, but there existed a hint of disgust somewhere.

The android could help him. Camden disregarded everything he'd done. He ignored the kidnapping, hurting Gear, knocking him out, and bringing him back to this hellhole. All of it would be forgiven if he helped him. The military-grade black eyes watched Camden as Morgan leaned down to embrace him.

Morgan whispered in his ear, "I missed you."

Camden wanted to cry, wanted to scream, to kick and to break anything. But Camden focused only on the android. He looked with pleading eyes. The tall, military machine watched the psychiatrist with confusion but shook his head as if it didn't matter what he saw. He banished that panic. "Please," Camden whimpered, "help me." The android looked down at him. Camden saw a flash of something that wasn't there. It looked like pity. Androids didn't feel pity, and they certainly didn't show it.

"Why are you asking him for help?" Dr. Morgan squeezed him, bringing a cracking sound. Camden's breath caught in his throat. No bones were broken—yet. "You think they have souls, right? Well, this one will show you the opposite."

The android cast his eyes away. Disgust holographed in that hallucination. Camden, for a second, saw that six-foot-four giant killing machine as a small kid avoiding the repercussions of his actions. His face was indifferent, blocking out emotions as he had seen Gear do so well. The android swiveled his jaw like he was testing an idea. Camden squeezed his eyes shut, blocking out the abandonment. There was no escaping this. Gear was out of commission, and Rave would never be able to find him.

Morgan pushed him onto the ground. Teeth, oddly sharp, dug into his jaw. Camden screamed. Claws dug into his shoulders to keep him from thrashing. He couldn't take it anymore. He couldn't stand the pain, the running, the fear. Camden wanted it all to end; he wanted to be free. He bashed his head back into the concrete floor. Then again. Hands shot up to hold his head still. Morgan pulled away to look at him.

"No, no, no." Morgan shook his head. "You don't get to go that way. You're not allowed to die." Camden's ragged breath shook, and he sniffled. He was so tired. Morgan procured a small vial and pressed it into his arm. "Just rest for a bit. You'll come back to your senses after some time. You'll see."

Camden felt the high after a second of it entering his bloodstream. He felt his pain slip away as he rested his head against the floor. The drugs didn't take the pain away but muddied his brain so well that he believed there wasn't any to begin with. They didn't help with the real torture. Morgan stood and turned to the other, who was avoiding any sudden movements.

The psychiatrist's newfound demeanor reflected calm and dangerous. "I'll pay a reasonable price as soon as you offer it."

"Okay," the android complied.

Camden didn't hear the sound of a door breaking free from its hinges and Rave's voice scream down at them, "Let Camden go, or I'll kill you!"

Δ Δ Δ

Infinite heard the female voice echoing down from the main part of the house. He looked over his shoulder at the doorway that led up and out of the basement. It was the H1A45 model that had run him in circles for hours as he searched for R8P1030. A grin spread on his face. This he would do for free. Turning, he went up the steps to see the erotically dressed android standing atop the staircase. She backed up so he could come through. Then she got into a fighting stance, right arm dominant. Fin grinned at her, leaning on one leg. "You're going to fight me? Is this because I trashed the R8P?"

The child-rearing model known as Rave glared through her open-palm stance. Her neon-colored nails almost made him laugh. She had military programs in that head of hers, so he knew not to underestimate her. Yet it was so cute to see such a soft, old model face up against his hard outer armor. "I want the human you took. Give him back."

Fin raised an eyebrow. "What is with you civilian models and throwing yourselves away? You know you can't win. Why kill yourself over a human?"

She smirked, a pitying look that sent burning rage through his wires. "You can't know, and I feel sorry for you. Already the best, so you can't get any better. Already know everything, so you can't learn anything new." He took the bait, calculating that she wouldn't be fast enough to dodge the blow. He jabbed for her collarbone port. She knocked his hand to the side, causing him to barrel forward a bit. He adapted and quickly refaced her. The civilian android was faster than he expected. A rush of cooling fluid sped through his tubes as his system heated from the excitement for the fight.

He jabbed again, this time for her cooling tanks. She swatted him to the side again, but he was prepared. He threw another jab with the other hand. She pushed off his first jab and spun on the outside of his guard. His second jab missed. Calculations flooded him as he tried to figure out her movements. She swept low, knocking his perfect stance off balance. Then she went for a place under his ribcage. How did she know his higher-strength backup cooling tank was there? He hit her hand, changing its course as he fell on the floor. His dark eyes watched as she spun back around with the grace of a dancer. He let out some exhaust. "Impressive."

She didn't answer. Her rainbow hair settled from the spin. She was like a tiger. He pushed off from the ground and leaped back to his feet. This time, he would be ready. They circled counterclockwise as he tested her parrying with a few jabs and double jabs. He calculated her probable maximum speed given her series's cooling system and frame melting point. He wasn't sure he wanted to cause her to melt down. This was the best fight he'd ever had against a civilian android. She was waiting for him to make a mistake. She was on the defensive. Smart. Maybe he could force her to make one first. He kicked low, aiming for her back leg to throw her off balance. She lifted it, twisted, and drove it into his gut, pushing him back with a huff.

"What the hell are you?" he said, running diagnostics on the hit.

Her intense eyes bore into him. "Don't you already know?" Then she dove forward. Bringing up his hands, he prepped for the hit. She flipped off the floor in a cartwheel. He calculated her trajectory. Got her. He drove his hand in an uppercut to catch her in the back before she reached him. Hands caught his, and she twisted her body around him, using his immovable arm against him. She bent and snaked low. She wrapped her legs around his midsection and spun around him to his back. Grappling his neck, she pinched at the wires under his silicone. Then she tore them out. Fin cried out as his calculations halted. Reaching over his shoulders, he flipped her over onto the floor. She grunted as her system received the shockwave.

He stumbled back, away from her, grasping at his neck, trying to reconnect cords that were not there. His heads-up display blinked out of existence. Where were his programs? He couldn't see them. She stood up, watching his panic.

"You'll see one day," she said as she cooled her circuits down, "once you stop relying on your superiority to explain things."

"How dare you!" He shook his head. He could sense his programs running, but he did not understand what they were and what they meant. There was nothing telling him anything. All he saw was her face. He was in the dark. Was this how civilian androids ran? How did they even work? "I'll kill you!" He charged, but he had no indicator of what she would do. He couldn't see the signs of her innate movements. Was she going to dodge? Was she going to swat him? What about a backflip? He couldn't figure out what his calculations were telling him. She drove a fist into his jaw from below. An uppercut. He felt like he should have seen it in her stance, but he was blind without the heads-up display. Fin collapsed at her feet. He knew defeat when he saw it, but feeling it was something else entirely. His system buzzed from the forced disconnect from the blow. His head would need to be reattached to move his body. Fin let out a sigh. This sucked.

△ △ △

Rave turned toward the basement door to see Dr. Morgan clap. A collected smile plastered on enraged her. This man tortured Camden and now smiled like she had just done him a favor. "Let him go."

"I will never let him go." Morgan opened his arms as if to offer her an idea. "Surely, you know that by now."

"He's a human being that deserves happiness." Rave tried to reason with him, though she prepared her programs for what needed to be done.

Morgan sighed. "We both love him the same way, don't you see?" Rave contorted a face of disgust. He could never understand how to be human, and she could never understand him. "He means the world to me. He is the center of everything."

Rave shook her hand and set back into a fighting stance. "I will force you to free him if I have to."

His mouth spread wide, wider than she thought was possible. "You think any force in the universe can separate me from him? Nothing can. Not even you."

She charged at him and tackled him. They tumbled down the stairs. A sickening thud started the flow of blood on the bottom step. Rave raised her head, prying herself out of his grip. His dying eyes stared at the ceiling above them. Choked noises sounded in his throat as he twitched. Then he stilled. Rave killed a human. She ignored the system issue as she walked through the doorway to Camden's side. She cradled his head in her arms. His brown eyes couldn't quite see her. She stroked his hair. "I love you, Cam. I will always protect you." Then her system powered down as the emergency protocol dialed the police.

Δ Δ Δ

The police station was mostly quiet. This side of the station held androids, so the prisoners didn't have to be locked up or fed. Along the back wall, behind a heavy set of glass windows, the arrested were hung up to charge stations. Two others besides Rave were hooked up. Gear scanned her for damage, but she'd sustained none. Thank goodness. Desmond and Clue both came to the same conclusion. An android stood behind the desk and tilted his head as he attempted to identify the guests. "Identification, please." Clue blinked at him, and the android changed his tune. "Forgive me. How may I help you?"

Desmond leaned on the counter and pointed toward Rave. "That one there. I want her released."

"That will need cleara—" he began, but Clue locked eyes with the android over Desmond's shoulder. "Right away."

The police android, whose nametag read Bitter, walked back behind the sliding door to the prison area. He unhooked Rave's collarbone port and ran his fingers along her temple. Seeing her depowered state, the vulnerability within him made itself more prevalent. Gear unclenched his hands after realizing they'd locked up. There was something wrong with his arm muscles. They locked up his fists at random times.

Rave came online with her color-changing eyes starting up in their default white. Frantically, she looked around for something, grabbing at air. The officer rested his hand on her shoulder and said something to calm her down. It worked, and she followed him to the front. Her eyes locked on Gear, and a smile crested her lips. A need to seize hold of her overcame him, but he couldn't process a reason. Clue's heavy hand shoved him from behind, having been in his head a second ago, and he fell forward toward her. He caught his balance a few inches away from her. She seemed to debate something as her fingers twitched beside her legs.

She said, "You're okay."

"So are you," he said. Desmond made a noise behind them, but they both ignored him. "What happened?"

Clue stepped forward. "I would also like the details."

Rave eyed Clue with an almost unfriendly glance that surprised Gear. But she nodded and offered him her hand. He took hold and leaned down to kiss it. Gear said, "Where's Camden?"

Clue pursed his lips as he let go of Rave's hand. The officer approached to offer them information. "The human at the scene wasn't in the database, but we sent him to First Support to wait out the drugs he'd been given. He also had several wounds that needed to be looked at by a doctor."

"What about Dr. Morgan?" Gear asked.

Clue answered, "She killed him."

"Actually," Officer Bitter continued, "there was no body at the crime scene. There was a little blood, and when we ran it in the database, no one came up. With no body, Ms. Rave hasn't committed a crime."

"Even though I know I killed him?" Rave asked through a bit of a daze.

Clue placed a hand on her shoulder. "It's because you could have been tampered with. I'd like to know about the T series, if you don't mind."

Bitter took another command via eye contact. "Yes, of course. Infinite is in the back. He's sustained critical damages, and we've called a mechatronologist to receive him."

"That's unnecessary." Clue's lips creased. "We'll take him. Take me to him."

"Yes, sir."

"Oh, Gear, one more thing." Clue turned back. Gear looked up and waited for his response. "The human. I'd watch him. From what I've gathered, he seems unstable."

Gear's face darkened as Clue headed past the doors to the back of the station. A hand interlocked with his own, forcing it to unclench. She leaned in close to speak softly. "Bring him home."

14 ▎

Blink

First Support Emergency Hospital contained muted walls painted thickly in creams and off whites. Humans eyed Gear with interest from the waiting room chairs as if nothing else could satiate their need for drama. Gear wouldn't say he provided any drama or even an ounce of hysteria, but the woman at the desk made parts of him clench up he wasn't aware could.

"I'm not seeing a Camden Smith in our system," she said with animated features. The woman's name was Claire Wild, and she worked the front desk as she had for the last thirteen years. Gear's facial recognition filed all her information, and her side hobbies included the artistic medium of digital scrapbooking. He didn't need to actually dig for that, since her desk frames included cycling pages of her work. It was beginning its second cycle by the time she asked the same question for the third time. "What's his date of birth?"

"I've answered that twice already. If you didn't find him the first time, you won't find him." Gear dug his fingers into his leg. Claire hummed a tune only she could hear, though Gear recognized the song by its tempo and the notes she attempted to make as new and popular. "He should have just arrived a few hours ago."

"We had a John Doe come in around three. Do you think he could be your guy?" she said.

Gear wanted to rip something, but his programs thought it inefficient. She could have brought the unnamed patient up earlier, but it probably didn't cross her mind. "Yes. Where is he?"

Claire leaned over the counter to point down the hall. "Take a left, and he'll be the fourth curtain past the double doors. The number is seven."

With as much enthusiasm as he could manage, which was negligible, he said, "Thank you."

After following the instructions, he arrived at the curtain labeled seven and hesitated. It only lasted a nanosecond, but it didn't go unnoticed. Gear pulled the curtain back to find Camden wrapped in fresh bandages and an IV hooked to his arm. The man slept peacefully as the saline solution fixed his dehydration. Gear breathed the exhaust from his lips; visible hot air floated upward, blurring his vision for a second. The clock on the wall above him marked the time at five forty-eight in the morning. Minutes ticked by—six, six thirty, seven. Gear stood unmoving as he waited for the sun to bring the waking hours. Camden didn't stir once.

Gear spent the time processing data, both what had transpired the previous day and what Clue had said. Sean Quinn, or as Gear knew him, Robert Smith, had faked his death less than a year before Camden's birth. Through all his memories, all the times he spent in the garage with Robert, he searched for something relating to the man Clue showed him. It was possible he destroyed the research, fearing it would bring harm to his family.

Something didn't fit, no matter how much he processed. The missing variables not only created gaps in his programs but also kept him from defining constants. Where was Camden's mother? Robert married Elizabeth when Camden was twelve, but there was no record of him being married prior. Gear shifted his search to Sean Quinn and found the woman he searched for. The soft features of

Camden's mother looked back at Gear, as did her date of death. The date was the same as Camden's date of birth. Gear's eyes flicked to the sleeping human; he wondered if Rave knew this information. Something in his programs told him Rave didn't need to know.

Still, this additional information didn't give any new equations to figure the many unknown variables swimming around. He started another search when the curtain drew back and the nurse stepped in to check on him. A familiar voice halted all Gear's processes. "Hello again."

Gear jerked his head to look at the person he thought had been the nurse. Several errors blinked up as her features glitched. "What do you want? Can't you leave him alone?"

The woman stood next to the empty IV stand. All personality blocked him out. "You forget I am your employer. You also let him out of your protection. Not very good at this, are you?"

"I'm not a babysitter." Gear looked at the clock, which had stopped ticking. "He needed someone stronger."

"He looks fine to me," she said.

"Are you after what his father knew?" Gear glared back at the glitch and demanded at least one unknown to be known.

"In a way."

"He likely doesn't even know about it, so leave him out of this," Gear said.

"That's not your job," she said. "He isn't aware of it, but he needs to be. Why are you so determined to help him? It's just a job to you, right?"

Gear didn't understand his own processes. It was clear he protected Camden because it was his job, but Morgan was dead. His job was complete, so why did he know in every sensor, wire, and program in his entire vessel that this job would never end? The thing to do would be to take his pay and walk away, but Gear couldn't even open his mouth to ask for what was due. The fingers on his hands clenched and unclenched. He couldn't walk away. Gear couldn't find a single process or program that told him this wasn't the conclusion of his job. The information Sean Quinn hid from the world wasn't his concern. The job was to locate and protect Camden from Morgan. Morgan was dead. It was done.

Yet, his body wouldn't respond. Gear couldn't, he *wouldn't* leave Camden. Nothing made less sense than to stay, and nothing meant more than to stay. Gear said, "He's my brother."

The glitch had ended several seconds ago while Gear had reached the conclusion. The redacted woman had left when she finished her sentence, but Gear hadn't paid it any mind. He didn't notice the ticking of the clock starting up again. In those quiet moments, Gear felt all his sensors, all his wires line up with human emotions. This emotion, newly named, had been in him since he was hardly a year old.

△ △ △

Camden woke in a painless stupor and could have almost forgotten the previous night, had he not woken in a hospital. Gear, standing by, said, "Sleep well?"

There was a crack on Gear's lip down to his jaw. The silicone had dried out from his expelling of coolant. Sitting up, Camden said, "Gear? How are you up and running?"

"Rave has interesting friends. They fixed all the critical issues."

Camden rubbed his eyes and felt compression gloves over his bandages. "That's impressive. It would've taken me at least a day or two to fix you. What time is it? How long have you been here?"

"Three twenty in the afternoon. Since five."

"You've just been standing there for—" Camden paused as he counted the hours on his fingers. "Ten hours?" It would have been quicker to count backward instead.

"Yes."

"Why?" Camden drew out the question in disbelief.

"It's my job," Gear answered.

"Still," Camden plucked at his eyelashes, trying to drag crusty sleep from them. "It must've felt like an eternity."

Gear looked away. The excessive drugging blurred the ghost of his face, and Camden tried to wipe away the fuzz. "No," Gear said, "I'm an android."

"Androids still feel time," Camden glowered, "maybe even more so."

"I had a lot to process," Gear said, then looked back at Camden, "which is what I'd like to discuss with you."

"Okay." Camden waited.

"I knew your father," Gear started and continued when Camden didn't respond, "I had something happen a long time ago, and your father fixed me up. You were six. So we've met before."

Camden raised an eyebrow. He didn't know where this was coming from, where it was going, or even the importance of it. Gear waited as if expecting some kind of indication, "Okay? Go on."

"He was the one who gave me the Sherlock program," Gear said, and Camden opened his mouth wide, remembering why that name had seemed to touch a nerve with him. His father designed several programs, and it surprised Camden he hadn't remembered it sooner. Gear continued, "There's something else. I don't know if you know this, but your father used to work for a company before you were born. While he was there, he discovered something."

"Something?" Camden asked. His father had known a lot about things related to all androids and their designs, but he had never talked about his prior job description. Camden knew that he hadn't been a mechatronologist his whole life, since he was one of the first ones to come about. He figured he had once worked for some android development company, but he never really asked.

"That's the issue. No one knows what he discovered, and it may be the reason you're in danger," Gear said.

"What?" Camden shook his head. "No, I'm only in danger because my psychopathic psychiatrist went full sadist on me."

"Did Dr. Morgan ever ask you about your father? Did he ever seem overly interested in his work?"

"No. My father was already pretty sick when I went to Morgan. I only really talked about that, and he never wanted to hear about anything off subject." Camden hadn't noticed he'd raised his voice. "What are you even saying? What do you mean my father discovered something?"

The hallucination of Gear's face looked nervous, unsure but the whole thing was too blurry. His actual demeanor was stoic and confident. "Someone is after you because of the information your father hid. She hired me to find you."

"Yeah, but only Morgan ever attacked me." Camden said. "You said *she*. Tell me about this woman that hired you. Maybe I know her."

"I can't," Gear said. "Every time she contacted me, I couldn't scan her. She hacked my software and prevented me from identifying her."

A chill went down Camden's spine, but he didn't know why. "She never showed you her face?" When Gear shook his head, Camden felt nauseous. "Never gave you a name?" Gear shook his head again. Camden took a deep breath to steady his rising panic attack. Where was all this nervousness coming from? With a jolt, he remembered why he was in the hospital. "Wait, where's Morgan? Did you get him arrested?"

"Morgan's dead."

Camden felt the world spin as he tied down the balloons of thought fleeing him. Morgan was dead? "How?"

"Rave. She took down that other android as well."

All those years, all those sessions, hadn't Morgan only tried to help him? No, he couldn't forget what kind of person he was. Morgan had mentally tortured him for years under the pretense of help. Only after it had grown into full-blown physical torture had Camden learned that therapy wasn't supposed to be torture. Still, he never wanted him to die. Deep down, he almost felt as though Morgan was his only friend. It was a horrible and abusive friendship, but Camden never had many friends to begin with. Why did it feel like he'd just lost a friend?

Camden looked into the dark-gray pressure gloves as if he could see through them down to the evidence of torture. All that pain had made him hope for death. Morgan offered no out, no proper explanation. It was a game to him, just a sick child playing a game. It had always been a game to them, but Camden always got the short end of the stick each time.

Gear's hand pressed against the top of Camden's, and Camden looked up at Gear's unchanging face. The hallucinations brought one of human comfort. Camden said, "Thanks. I don't know what's wrong with me. I hated him, but I didn't want him to die."

Camden felt his voice croak near the end and squeezed his eyes shut. He should feel relief, but all he felt was anger and sadness. Why couldn't anything in his life be normal? Why did everyone around him always die? Every single death ripped a hole in him, and he felt so alone. Heavy arms wrapped around his shoulders. He knew it was Gear, but he couldn't focus on anything but how utterly miserable he was. Was this what he had wanted when he went off the medications? Was this what it was like to be alive? This was horrible. This was cold and lonely and like being flayed from the inside.

Δ Δ Δ

Camden shook as Gear held on to him. He wasn't sure why he did it, but he knew he needed to. It was normal to value life, but was it normal to value one that had caused you so much pain? Gear did not understand, but he did not let go. He let Camden mourn, for whatever reason, even if he did not know it. Gear didn't need to know.

When Camden had calmed down enough, Gear let go and looked at his red, leaking face. "Stay with us." Camden coughed a late sob as his puffy eyes stared at Gear with such intensity that Gear faltered. "I'm sure Rave would love to have you around."

After some time, Camden nodded. "Okay," he said and checked out of the hospital. Gear drove them back to the loft, where the door was reattached to the wall. The splintered wood would need replacing, but it didn't have priority. Rave wasn't home, and the loft was quiet.

"You can sleep in Rave's bed. It'll be more comfortable for you," Gear said, helping Camden walk on his newly bandaged foot. Camden said nothing as they entered the messy red room, and he sat down on the bed. After a few moments of staring blankly, Gear turned to leave.

"You said you knew my father," Camden said, and Gear froze. "Your face mold ..." Gear felt every system hesitate its calculations. What was Camden going to say? Gear had appreciated his father, that's it. No, that's not it. Camden's father meant the world to him. He wanted to be like him: caring and wise. Gear had become neither. "It looks like it'll need a touchup from that cracking." Gear turned back around to see a sad smile pressed into Camden's face. He knew.

Somehow, Gear knew that those eyes saw everything. Those eyes haunted him in his memories, and now they knew him in life.

Gear fled the room.

For the next couple hours, Gear sat on the couch in his place, replaying the memory of Camden's haunting eyes. The windows echoed the same eye color and even the same shape, but they did not hold the same knowledge. Gear touched one of his eyes as he watched his reflection. How could something that looks so similar be so different?

Rave entered the loft and said, "Hey, is he asleep?"

Gear looked over his shoulder at her. She was quieter than normal. Her hair, still luminescent rainbow in hue, hung over her shoulders. Her eyes, hazel now, watched him as she walked over to join him on the couch.

She sat down and said, "What's wrong?"

"I don't know," Gear answered as every question he thought he knew the answer to rewrote itself. Every equation about the world he had filed now had new parameters. He could quickly fix and answer those new equations, but even by then, they'd have new variables. Everything was unattainable, and even his Sherlock program seemed worthless to answer anything.

"What do you mean? Is Camden all right?" she asked.

"He's asleep in your bed." Gear could answer that question. "But I think I may be broken."

Rave stared at him for a long time and offered her hand. Gear looked at it, then back up to her softened eyes. Those eyes knew things he could never hope to. Everyone around him knew everything, and he had nothing. The world he had once thought was a sphere spinning in infinite space now looked more jagged and the space less infinite than what he didn't know. "You are not broken," Rave said, "you are alive."

The words, so foreign, so incorrect, resonated with all definitions. A week ago, he would have scoffed at her, but he needed an answer to any of these questions. If only one answer was exactly what it was. "I am alive?"

Rave smiled. "It's about time you woke up."

"What do you mean?" Gear asked. "And why does everything ... feel?"

She scooted closer, still holding out her hand, "That's how you know everything is working. I've waited so long for you that I worried you'd never come around."

She wrapped her arms around him, offering his body a million fresh ways to recognize pressure. His arms raised on their own, accepting the hug. It differed from the other times. This one was more everything. For a long time, Gear thought only humans needed comfort. That androids only existed to suit the needs of humans and that they never needed to feel. Thinking about that, it looked like a redundancy. Humans needed comfort, and androids could provide it. To feel was a strange phenomenon, and yet so extreme.

All these years, Gear refused to let himself feel anything. He told himself he didn't need it, and it hindered his work. Anytime he felt anything, he would drown it. He would focus only on statistics and calculations. He didn't want it, but now it seemed to offer answers, or at least it offered a lack of need for them.

He pulled back and looked at Rave's face, and without calculating, he sent her the memory. Her eyes glazed for a second as she watched his decades-old experience. Then her hazel eyes saw him, and her face replicated pain. *His pain.* Written all over her face. A calm peace washed through him. Letting go of something he'd unnoticeably hidden from himself and everyone else brought a strange absolution. With her reaction, he could accept his own emotions as what they were. The world, which exact shape it took meant little to him, and the space beyond could be an infinite of infinites. In this moment, all Gear could accept was peace and the unnamed emotion he now knew the name of.

A scream brought both of them back to the physical. Rave and Gear jumped to their feet. It was Camden. Rave followed as Gear charged into the room to find something he couldn't process.

Δ Δ Δ

Camden felt the claws dig into him, waking him up. It stood over him, the creature from his dream, but this time it didn't have his face. The dark creature's big, black eyes reflected Camden's terror back at him. He had to be dreaming. He screamed in pain as it lifted him up by the holes it made in his shoulders. *This is a dream. This isn't happening.* Grabbing the wrists of the creature, he felt it. It felt real, but it just couldn't be. The face lacked all color, all light, and had no features but the bulbs of eyes. Then it opened its mouth. It leaned in, many layers of teeth showing, and it spoke to him. "I can't take it anymore."

The claws on one hand pulled from his shoulders and skirted down his cheek, drawing a line of his blood. The giant black eyes stared into his face, absorbing all of his facial expressions. Camden could see everything the creature saw in those black mirrors. His panic, his shaking. His fear. This face had no hologram, no ghost of emotions. Everything it felt was reflected so perfectly on its face. This face. It didn't seem possible for it to show emotions, but the air tinged with its bloodlust. He knew it well.

Gear burst into the room and stared blankly. The hallucination of pure confusion ghosted over his real face. Camden reached for him, begging that this couldn't be happening. "Help me!" he cried.

The creature turned to see the android and hissed, "You can't have him."

Gear was processing. It was taking too long. Camden cried out again, "Gear, help me, please!"

Rave burst into the room and tackled the creature without hesitating. Camden was thrown to the floor. She punched at its jagged features, but it kicked her off. She thumped into the wall and was back on her feet as fast. Its long, spider-like arms hoisted upward. "You!" it roared.

Camden clutched his bleeding shoulders and crawled toward the corner of the room. This wasn't happening. This couldn't be happening again. *Again?* Had this happened before? Rave was back on the creature, wrangling it like a wild boar. Gear concluded his calculations and dragged Camden from the floor. He grunted from strain as Gear pulled him from the room.

"You can't keep him from me!" it screamed.

Gear squeezed his shoulders, trying to halt the blood flow a bit. Camden gasped and choked out, "Is this actually happening? Can you see that thing?" Gear nodded as he withdrew his hands, pulled the silicone back, and heated the metal beneath up to a burning hot. Then he pressed them back into the holes as Camden bit into his shirt. Necessary as it was, burning the wound made him want to pass out.

"Camden, is that Blink?" Gear asked with fierce stoicism on his indifferent face.

"What?" he yelled, still coming off the burn shock.

"Focus." Gear grabbed him and shook him. "When you were six years old, your imaginary friend, who you named Blink, attacked you. When you were fifteen, your friend was punctured full of holes right in front of you. You just received two of those same holes. Is. That. Blink?"

Camden gaped at him in silent horror at the insanity of what he was asking. Gear's straight face told him he reached some kind of answer that had reflected even in the hallucination. Was it possible for an android to go crazy? When he was six ... When he was fifteen ... This *had* happened before. Camden recalled the creature that attacked his best friend. The same one? Had it not been a hallucination? Had he ever really hallucinated? "This ... it can't be real."

Another series of shakes. "Really? You're going to deny that the thing that bit you as a kid, murdered your friend, tore holes in you, and is currently duking it out with Rave is real? Wake up. This is happening. I don't know what this is, but you need to remember. You need to remember what that thing is. And you need to tell me before it rips us all to shreds."

Camden remembered the alley. He had been a bit drunk, but he remembered it. It seemed like the shadows tore holes into his friend, let him drop to the ground and then had said ... What did the shadows say? When he was six, had he really had an imaginary friend? Blink ... Blink ...

Oh ... right, Blink. His best friend—

△ △ △

"Let's play a game. I'll throw you the ball, and you throw it back," Camden said to the thing in the closet. He threw the ball. Reaching down, the little critter chewed on the ball. "No, you're supposed to throw it back." It blinked enormous eyes at him, then crawled out of the darkness. Its many layers of teeth didn't bother Camden. Its big, dark eyes were all he noticed. It handed the ball back to him, and he grinned. "Let's be friends."

He came home from school and ran to his room to cry. He couldn't let his dad see him like this. The kids at school had been mean to him. They had spat on him when he called out what he saw. Why did they put on false faces? Why did they lie to each other? It was crowd logic. They were mean to him because he knew when they cheated. Just because he could read them didn't mean he didn't want to play. He loved to play, and they wouldn't let him. He just wanted friends.

"Cam?" The creature crawled from the closet and nuzzled him. "What's wrong?"

"They got mad at me because I knew Jax was cheating. Then they said they didn't want to play with me anymore. They all knew, but they didn't care. Why did they lie?" Camden cried into his blankets.

"He's a bully. You don't need them," the creature said. "You have me, Cam. I'll always play with you."

Camden looked at the creature's gigantic eyes. "Thanks, Blink, you always cheer me up. You're my only friend."

"I'll always be your friend." Blink grinned his layers and layers of tiny teeth.

"I'll always be yours too."

Camden checked the closet; no Blink. He checked under the bed; no Blink. Where was that critter? Maybe Dad had seen him. He went to ask. Oh, he didn't check Dad's room. He opened the closet in the master bedroom, and Blink sat there huddling. "Hey, Blink, let's play." Blink didn't answer. Reaching out, he pulled on the critter, but it shoved him off. "Hey, come on. Let's play."

Something was wrong, but Camden knew they could work through it. They talked about everything with each other. He reached to tug again, and Blink snapped at his arm. Camden didn't respond to the pain. He only saw his friend's pained eyes. He needed to help him, but then it hurt. Camden let out a scream. Blink's eyes widened even further. Surprise, terror, fear, and then ... something else. Desire.

Δ Δ Δ

"Blink ..." Camden said, completely calmed down. "I can't believe I forgot."

"What?" Gear shook him. "Do you remember something?" Camden pushed out of his grip and stood. Gear still sat in confusion, trying to process. Camden walked back into the room to watch as Rave lost the upper hand. It smashed her into the wall, and her system clicked off. Her body crumpled inside the busted concrete wall; the dresser was in shards, and the clothes still resembled a kicked-over trash can. Gashes riddled her silicone and the hard metal beneath. Camden couldn't believe she continued to fight in her condition. Her body ran out; her system had to shut down. The creature raised its clawed hand to tear her apart.

"Blink," Camden called. The creature froze, turned, and stared. He didn't know what to say or where to start. A wave of despair washed over him as he couldn't say a word.

It lowered its clawed hand to the floor and slowly padded up to him. Blink was much bigger than it had been when he was a kid. All was relative, though. To Camden, it was always this size. It had just grown with him. "You remember," it said.

"You hurt me," Camden said. "You've hurt me so much, Blink."

The creature shriveled a bit and snapped, "You replaced me! I just wanted it to go back to just us, but you forgot me ... and you replaced me."

"They told me you weren't real. They made me believe you weren't real." Camden calmly reached out to touch the creature. It shied away.

"I thought I just needed to be close to you. I thought becoming that psychiatrist would be enough. I could be close, and it was for a while, but you started to remember me. I could see it on your face, and then you spoke of that dream. I couldn't take it anymore. I needed you. I was so lonely without you," it whimpered.

Camden looked up at it and knew exactly what he saw. He understood it. Every single thing it ever did made sense. The loneliness they felt always vanished when they were together. That was how it always was, but Camden couldn't forget all that happened. Blink was not the childhood friend he knew; it had killed his friend out of jealousy, and it killed Dr. Morgan, who had probably been a nice person. Camden knew it would take more, and he knew it would kill anyone he ever cared about or needed. It would kill Gear. It would kill Rave.

Camden wrapped his arms around the thing that terrorized him all his life, and he accepted his fate. "Then take me," he said.

"No!" Gear screamed as he started forward. Blink snapped back into the situation and shoved Camden aside. The creature lunged and prepared to rip the android apart, but Camden grabbed the creature's arm, pulling Blink back and down with him.

Camden didn't cry out, just grunted when Blink's claws pierced his chest. Blink stared absently for a second, while Gear froze in his steps. "Cam, no," Blink whimpered as he pulled the claws out and cradled his head. "Don't leave me."

Camden felt a strange peace, despite all the numb pain as it pounded his head. The fatal blow seemed like pricking a finger compared to what he'd faced. Despite all that happened and what Camden had been willing to do, he felt like he was cheating. Then he didn't care. The creature stroked his cheek almost affectionately. Camden's own blood on those fingers. His vision faded of color, but he saw a figure behind Blink. It was a shadow shaped as a woman, or maybe just a human. Maybe it was an android. He couldn't be sure.

Δ Δ Δ

"No." Blink held Camden's dying body as he lost consciousness. Gear watched in horror. Then he saw the shadow. It was as if light could not escape the shape. The surrounding air bent slightly as it walked toward the grumbling creature.

She stood behind the creature and spoke only to it. Gear knew the voice. "I told you not to touch what's mine. Now look what you've done."

The creature shook but didn't turn around right away. In a rage, it lashed its claws out at the absent space that was the shadow. "You did this! I had him. He remembered."

"You had nothing," she said. "You keep killing him. I've already grown tired of fixing your messes. Do you see how this won't ever work out in your favor?"

"Bring him back," Blink demanded. "You did it before."

"Why?"

Gear had trouble following, but this last thing she said angered him. He felt his circuits burn red hot as the electricity flowed through them. He was about to interject, but Blink spoke. "Why did you do it the first time? You can do it again."

"I did it because I could. Things work differently here. You understand that, at least." She waved her arm, and it bent the space. "Besides, in a moment, it will all be irreversible. What will you do now?"

"Bring him back," Blink repeated, faintly this time. "Use me. Just save him."

The silence so deafening, his robotic ears rang, Gear froze in space and time, waiting for the answer. Gear couldn't understand anything, even if he tried, so he watched as a helpless bystander yet again.

She finally spoke. "Do you know what it is you're asking?"

Blink looked down at Camden. "He's my best friend." Then he looked back up as if that was the answer. She offered him an empty hand, and Blink placed his talons in it. The creature was sucked into her empty space like he'd never been there at all. She looked down at Camden and leaned down to touch him. If one touch could suck a creature from existence, then he couldn't let her touch Camden. Gear launched forward, but she bent the room's length. He was so far away, he'd never make it in time.

"Calm down," she said as she brought forth something from within her empty space. It looked sort of like a shard of glass. It floated off where her hand would be if she wasn't absent space, and a similar one rose out of Camden's chest to connect with it. The pieces made a proper shape, though he couldn't count the sides, even with his scanners. It lowered and dissipated upon touching his skin. Camden's body mended like a lattice of skin lacing over an invisible mesh. Skin reached over the gaps and healed like his own cells had learned to fly. Where holes bled, now contained old scars under torn clothes. Camden would live.

Gear watched in baffled confusion as the impossible unfolded before him. None of his systems seemed to be working properly. Nothing was running, but he was sure he was still powered on. Then the shape looked at him. He knew it did, though she had no face. Somehow, he knew. It approached him. Gear backed up a step, but stopped, remembering the warped room. She stopped in front of him. "I destroyed the anomaly. Your job is now complete."

"What?" he asked. "What about the information? What about Sean Quinn?"

She was silent and unmoving for a few seconds. He figured she was debating something, but he doubted he'd ever know what. "That is for you to find out, if you wish to. I do not seek that information. I already know it. It was this creature I wanted."

"Blink."

"That is what you call it," she said.

"What are you?" he asked, already knowing she wouldn't answer that.

It didn't surprise him when she answered, "That is not for you to know."

"Who is it for? Him?" He felt anger, yes, anger. He could name this emotion, though he wasn't sure why he felt it. Camden had been through enough, and Gear didn't want this information to bring him any more suffering. "He's been through enough."

"As have you," she said, "but you both have more to do."

He opened his mouth to say more, but she vanished. He hadn't even blinked. She was just ... gone. Surveying his two damaged but living friends, he tried to process everything that had just happened. He knew that if he started this process to understand, it would last indefinitely. Gear shut it down and called Clue.

15

Everything as We Know it

Camden's house was exactly how he left it. There was a bowl sitting in the sink full of murky water, and the book he'd been reading was left on the couch. His stuff was laid bare before him, but it seemed like it belonged to someone else. Had it only been three weeks? Camden pressed his fingers into a mark on the kitchen table. No memory of how it got there came to mind, but its existence was nostalgic. It felt like he was saying good-bye to someone he once knew.

Gear stepped inside and followed Camden from room to room to look at different things. His electronic eyes were more interested in old pictures that littered the walls. Camden had seen them so often that they blended into the background. The one Gear pulled from the wall was one taken eight years ago when he graduated from the mechatronologist program. His father, sick then, had shown up to congratulate him. Gear had found the last pleasant picture of his father before his death.

Camden started, "He was sick for so long. I don't even remember what it was like before."

Gear replaced the photo on the wall and turned to the rest of the room they were searching. The bedroom hadn't been touched since his father was hospitalized for the last time. "He was a good man," Gear said statically, but then stuttered when he realized Camden wanted more. "He struck me as the kind of human that cares about everyone."

"You know more about him than I do." Camden looked at his father's eyes in the photo once more before continuing his nostalgia tour. "I can't believe he never told me."

"He was protecting you," Gear said.

"From what?" Camden opened the closet and nudged out some old boxes. "We still don't know. All this junk is getting us nowhere. He didn't hide anything here; I would have found it already."

Gear said, "We should check the garage."

Camden scoffed and stood. "I know every inch of that garage. I'm telling you, there's nothing here. He probably destroyed it."

"I don't think so," Gear said and led the way down the steps into the basement garage. The android froze in the doorway after he switched the lights on.

Camden pushed past him. "What is it?" Gear's face flickered with the ghost of Camden's own: nostalgia. He chuckled and said, "You know, these hallucinations always fool me into thinking you have actual emotions. Come on, you wanted to check here."

Gear approached the console by the worktable. Camden figured he wouldn't need to give him the passcode or access, so he propped himself in his wheely chair and turned back and forth. Gear typed a few letters, and the screen clicked on to show recent work searches. The last android he cared for had been in an accident where she crushed her arm. He salvaged what he could and shipped the scrap to the manufacturer. She left with brand-new interior carbon-fiber muscles and new sensors. The silicone was usually the easiest to fix, though it took some time and precision to melt it and remold it. Gear's lip was still busted from the coolant. With a little time and the available tools, he could fix him good as new.

Camden pulled some tools off his bench and brought them to his worktable, startling Gear. "What are you doing?"

"I can remold your silicone, so I figured I'd do it while you dig through my files," Camden answered.

Gear looked down at the collection of objects and nodded. Camden took hold of his face and examined the dried and burned silicone fragments. He scraped them off with a scalpel. The crack ran from his lip down under his jaw, showing his sensors and the woven metal underneath. Taking some bonding agent, he glued what he could back together. Camden pulled up a specific tool, which could reverse cure and recure silicone. He pressed the needle point into the crack and carefully traced over it. If he made a mistake, the face design would need an entire remold. Camden didn't make a mistake in this part often. Only humans made little movements, so his subject didn't flinch. He wondered if they felt this part of the process.

Camden let his arm rest after a few millimeters to make sure he wouldn't accidentally jump. This was something that couldn't be rushed. He liked this part about as much as reshaping the carbon-fiber muscling. Gear hadn't moved, but the halo of his face quivered and looked on the verge of tears. "Did I hurt you?" Camden placed his hand on the android's shoulder in a panic.

The indifference on Gear's face gave him a raised eyebrow. "What?"

Camden backed away and remembered he needed another tool, one he would not use. He suddenly needed it that minute, or maybe he just needed to not be so embarrassed. "Nothing." Camden had spent his entire life pretending the hallucinations were real, and that got him into trouble with everyone. Sometimes it was hard to feign normal, especially when what he saw concerned him.

"It's not you," Gear said. "It's a good thing you are a mechatronologist."

Camden brought back over the tweezers he didn't need. "Well, I'm almost done. Have you found anything?"

"I haven't looked yet," Gear admitted.

Camden tilted his head and examined Gear's indifference. It could be mistaken for confidence if the ghost of embarrassment didn't invade Camden's eyes. Camden laughed and smacked Gear on the shoulder. "What are you even doing?"

"Thinking," Gear said.

"Sure," Camden said before he went quiet to focus on the last of the face crack. The bonding glided on, and it almost looked like new. "There we go. Are your sensors working underneath?"

"Camden," Gear said.

"Yeah?" He looked up at the horror on Gear's actual face. "What? What's wrong?"

"I found it," Gear said as his glazed brown eyes rolled to look at Camden's. "I don't know what this means."

"Show me." Camden turned the monitor, and an audio file came up. With his middle finger, he pressed the play button to hear his father's voice from over a decade ago.

"Hello again, Gear. If you're hearing this, then you've woken up. I hope you don't mind that I hid this with you. I stumbled upon something that I shouldn't have when I was synthesizing biomaterial for earlier android designs. What I discovered wasn't something I could understand alone, but its DNA-changing properties made it dangerous. With this log, I gave you the code to synthesize it again. I'll let you decide when humanity is ready for it.

"There is something else. I don't know how much time has passed, but if my son is still alive, I want you to find him. His name is Camden. You may have memories of him. There is something I need you to tell him for me. Tell him I'm sorry. Then tell him why.

"Before he was born, his mother, my wife, was dying. It was a rare situation, and the doctor was losing both her and the baby. I couldn't imagine it. I know it was stupid, unprofessional, and dangerous, but I exposed her to the biomaterial, and it did something unthinkable. Her body regenerated itself, though it was not enough. I don't know what happened, but we saved Camden. I believe she died saving him.

"Camden began showing signs of being able to see things that aren't there as early as he could see. He would smile and giggle in the crib when there was no one around. One time, I swore the crib was being rocked. I passed it off as my exhaustion, but he never got any better. It got worse as time went by. I told myself it was just his childish imagination, but he saw things in people themselves. It was as if he could read their minds or see their feelings. It didn't make him popular in daycare, and he never brought home any friends.

"I started logging things after a while, but I believe the synthesis affected him. I think what Camden sees is real, though I am afraid it will hinder him growing up. If what he sees is real, then this synthesis could change humanity. Camden may see into things none of us can, and that could open doors. But I worry about what you've seen, and I worry about the implications it will cause your kind. Maybe one day you will forgive humanity.

"Gear, I hope you find him. I hope you can help each other. Take care of him."

Camden and Gear didn't move for several minutes. Finally, Camden turned the chair toward the other. "Why didn't he tell me?" Gear reached out and placed a hand on his shoulder as he tried to process it all, "I don't understand. So, everything I've been seeing, all these things, even Blink is because of this biomaterial synthesis?"

"This code," Gear ran numbers, "it's related to humans, not androids. I'm running some simulations, but it looks like it could take years of trials. What happened to you may have been a one-time fluke."

"So, what was Blink, just some repercussion? Some creation of my own DNA?" Camden said.

Gear shook his head. "I don't know." He didn't know, and he wasn't sure he could ever know. It seemed like this was beyond him and his programs. The unknowns kept racking up, even as he ran simulation after simulation. More data meant less room for error, and yet the possibilities only increased.

Camden stood and ran a hand through his hair. After a few more minutes, he sighed. "I can't stand all this. I just want to not think anymore. You want to go play some games or something?"

"Games?" Gear looked at the human he considered the most important person in his life cycle. The troubles they faced could be disregarded for just a few hours while they focused on something trivial like games. Camden wasn't just offering a way to not think about the problems, he was offering Gear a place in his life. Gear smiled and nodded. They headed for the exit when it dawned on Gear. "I've never played any video games. That's more Rave's thing."

Camden ruffled Gear's hair, and the android felt some of his wires twist. The sensation was new yet comforting. Camden locked up his house and headed to the vehicle. He looked back when Gear didn't follow. "You have to start somewhere." Camden's face was exhausted. He hadn't slept well, and he still hurt. The hospital prescribed painkillers, but the purple under his eyes gave it all away. That and the decaying look in his eyes. Maybe one day Gear could see a day when everything would be all right.

16

We

Camden walked around the familiar darkness. The ground beneath him rippled like thick, black water. This calm, abysmal place he knew only in his dreams brought a strange, lonely sensation. Every time he'd been here, he had felt longing eyes or heard the heavy breathing of some monster he now knew was his old friend. Camden lived in terror in his sleeping hours and swam in tar in his waking ones. Blink, his friend, his enemy, his nightmare, had lived and dreamed in constant pain. Camden wasn't sure which one of them suffered more.

"Welcome home." Her voice filled the space.

He turned to see a human girl, no older than a teenager. All the times he had dreamed about her, he had never seen her. She hadn't once seemed young. "It's you."

"It's me," she said.

"This isn't a dream, is it?" Camden approached her. He was taller by half a foot.

She replied, "Was it ever a dream?"

Camden thought about all the new things he'd learned, and somehow, he felt like he had even more to learn. Something irregular tainted his DNA, and he wondered, "I'm not human anymore, am I?"

"Were you ever human?" she asked.

Camden recalled their first conversation in the hospital. She had been as curious about him as he had been about her. Now they seemed to know. "Are we the same?"

She smiled. "We are now."

"What does it mean?" he asked, half-expecting a worthless question again.

She turned around and headed back into the abyss. He watched her go, but then she looked over her shoulder. "Come, I'll show you."

ACKNOWLEDGEMENTS

I would like to thank Mam for telling me to save him, otherwise this book would have never come to be. I would like to thank Wary for coping with my insane ramblings during the process. Thank you, Joel, for editing this and translating it into proper language. Thank you, Richard, for telling me I had to write even if this wasn't the one you were talking about.

Many thanks to Alisha, Black, Thomas, Reid, and Bailey for being the friends who lifted me up. No matter how much time has passed, I know you as friends.